MW01148145

CONTENTS

COVERT BEAR

P.O.L.A.R.

CANDACE AYERS

LOVESTRUCK ROMANCE

Vilified by strangers,
Friendships aren't Heidi's forte.
Unless it happens to be with a displaced polar bear.

Hey, he's a great listener!

Alexei knows she's his mate.
But she refuses to date him.
All he wants is a chance.

And, as far as he can tell, there's only one way to get it—as a Covert Bear.

1

HEIDI

Jayden and Jonas Perez stared up at me with wide, blue puppy dog eyes and pouty little mouths that were turned down just the slightest bit at the corners. Skillfully, they'd perfected that hard-to-deny look before they'd even reached their third birthday and they used it for everything. It didn't matter how ridiculous their request was, when they shot me that look, my heart melted and I had a hard time denying either of them anything. Once, they'd almost convinced me to let them play in the street. I'd been scouting around looking for items to use as roadblocks before realizing I'd been played by two little masters. Those two had definitely figured out their superpower.

At that moment, they wanted the cup of coffee I was drinking. It took one stern *no* from me to have them both in tears. I knew the drill, though. Crocodile tears. Even so, my stomach knotted at their pitiful howls. The little con artists.

"What if I did give you coffee and it made you climb the walls? What would your momma say when she came home and found you on the ceiling?" I wagged my finger at them and drained my cup. "I don't think she'd be very happy with me if her precious baby boys were on the ceiling."

Jayden, the gigglier twin, broke protocol and laughed. Forgetting about my coffee, or more likely, seeing that it was gone and deciding to surrender the fight, he shoved his fingers in his mouth and turned to play with the blocks precariously stacked behind him. Jonas, the serious brother, had laser focus. He grabbed for my mug and scrunched up his face in a scowl when I slid it out of reach. He fell back on his diapered butt and let loose a full out wail. Jayden looked at him for all of two seconds before joining in.

I'd been watching them since they were days old, but I'd never grown a thicker skin against their cries. I scooped them both up—one in each arm—and carried them out to the porch. The warm sunshine and the sounds of the waves crashing always soothed them when they were tired and cranky. I sank into one of the deck chairs and held both boys against my chest until they stopped crying and fell asleep. Under the shade of a large porch umbrella, my feet kicked up, I let the beautiful sun and sea of Sunkissed Key relax me, too.

Maria Perez found us there when she arrived home from work a half an hour later. She took one look at her boys and smiled a bright, glowing smile. "You're the best. They don't nap for me."

I shifted and handed Jayden off to her. "Do you think the terrible twos will be over soon?"

Maria grinned wider. "Nope. Jake's parents tell me all the time about how Jake and Kyle were terrors from birth on. I'm geared up and ready for them to remain in their terrible twos until they turn eighteen and go off to college."

I shuddered. "Let's not talk about that. I don't like the idea of them ever being that old. Besides, it makes me think about how old I'll be when they reach adulthood."

"How old *you'll* be? Yeah, okay." Shifting Jayden to her right hip, she reached out and gently took Jonas from me, too. "I've got seven years on you. Do you know how much living happens in seven years? You'll still be young. I'll be practically be an old hag."

Rolling my eyes, I stood up and opened the door for her so we could all go back inside. "How was work?"

Maria worked at Mann Family Dentistry as a hygienist. Roger

Mann, the owner and main dentist at the clinic was a misogynist and usually made work difficult for Maria. Her face said it all. "He approached me about cutting my hours again this morning. Before our first patient. Told me that he'd understand if I needed to be at home with my kids more often. After all, kids need their mothers."

Scowling, I shook my head. "You've already cut back to half days. What does he expect from you?"

"I think he wants me out completely. I heard a rumor that there's a younger hygienist on the island. Cheaper and hotter." She sighed and rested the boys both on the couch. Looking up at me from her stooped over position, she said, "It's getting ridiculous."

I sighed, feeling for her. She'd been my best friend for over a decade and I loved her like a sister. I hated that she was having a hard time. More than that, her life had been a challenge for years. That much we had in common. "Have you thought any more about opening your own practice? You could do it. Just hire your own dentist. People love you and you have loyal patients who would follow you."

She shook her head and looked back at her boys. "Maybe when they're older."

I let it drop and headed into the kitchen. As part of my day job caring for the boys, I snuck in some extra TLC for Maria too. When she needed it, anyways. I had the time during the day and, honestly, I was glad to do it.

I'd just picked up some deli meat and freshly baked bread from Mann Grocery, owned by Roger Mann's brother, Ramsey. Ramsey was a lot nicer than Roger and didn't have a negative bone in his body. His wife, Martha, baked fresh breads and desserts daily and kept the island supplied. Their grocery store smelled like heaven on earth, every single day. I sliced a few pieces of bread and put together a sandwich with the deli meat, a slice of cheese, and some veggies.

"That looks so delicious." Maria sat down at the kitchen island and groaned when I pushed the plate over to her. "You're more treasured than gold, Heidi. I'm starved. Mayo?"

"Of course. On the top and bottom slice, just the way you like."

She took a hefty bite and moaned. "I love you."

I just rolled my eyes and put everything away. "Unless you need anything else, I'm going to head out. I need to clean my house before work tonight."

She waved me away. "Go. Thank you for this. And everything."

"Uh huh. I'll see you in the morning."

I left the house and took the beach path down to my house. Maria and the boys lived on Bluefin Boulevard and I could take the beach to avoid Coral Road and most of Gulfstream Lane. My house was at the end of Gulfstream Lane, on the beach. West Public Beach wasn't as populated as East Public Beach for whatever reason, but there were still a handful of people enjoying the sun and sand.

My house was a one story little beach bungalow on stilts. It'd weathered many hurricanes, including the most recent Hurricane Matilda. It looked almost like something the crew on Gilligan's Island would've built to live in, but it was quaint and beautiful to me. It needed a new coat of the dusty blue paint I'd chosen for it years earlier. The porch needed sealing against the ocean weathering, the roof was probably ready for an update, and the front door screeched like a banshee when you opened it. To me, it was home.

I had to jiggle the doorknob and use a hip thrust to get it to open, but the welcoming screech was so familiar that I usually replied to it. "Hello to you, too."

With a sigh, I looked around and got started cleaning.

2

ALEXEI

The ocean was cool against my large, furry body. Even with the sun beating down on me, I wasn't miserable. I dove under and swam down several feet, twisting and spinning until my lungs tightened and I had to come up for air. I loved the water... cool, freeing, and it did wonders toward making a 900 pound bear feel weightless.

I'd never liked being anywhere more than in the water. While the rest of the team was busy feeling tortured by our move to Sunkissed Key, I was just as happy as I'd been in Siberia. Well, maybe not when I was being forced to sit in the office, sucking up everyone's funk with the weird, "conditioned" oxygen. In the ocean, though, I was happy.

I'd taken the move better than everyone else. The ocean, bikini clad women, tacos... Things could've been so much worse. The only real downgrade was the work. Instead of conducting insertions and extractions, accomplishing covert, special ops missions, or capturing high-value enemy personnel, we were chasing down shop lifters and petty criminals and making sure locals and tourists didn't get drunk and punch each other out.

I felt like a babysitter. Worse, I felt like a useless babysitter. I missed stopping coups and assassination attempts, infiltrating terrorist cells, and protecting world leaders. Mostly. As I ducked under the water and swam down to the sandy bottom of the ocean floor, though, I felt like maybe babysitting wasn't all that bad of a career change.

My bear spotted a fish while we were down there and set off chasing it. He loved fishing. And eating. And, he especially loved filling his belly with fresh fish he'd caught himself. He was a simple bear. Hunt, eat, sleep, repeat. The stifling heat didn't even bother him all that much, as long as I took him for regular dips in the water.

Got an assignment. Rendezvous at the office. Serge's voice broke through my tranquility like a loudspeaker and interrupted fishing time. Serge was the task force Alpha.

The lucky fish were free to swim another day and my stomach grumbled. Oh, well. I'd eat later. Even though I swam in what was usually a secluded section of the island, I swam as far in as I could without being spotted by the locals before shifting. I kept a pair of swim trunks hooked to the side of the pier and easily slipped into them before emerging from the water and jogging along the sand down to the office.

Dripping wet with my lower body coated in a layer of sand by the time I got there, I made quick work of rinsing off with the outside shower head before going in to see what was up.

Serge stood in front of one of the window AC units, talking to the rest of the team. His eyes cut to me and he frowned. "About time you showed up."

I shrugged, not minding the reprimand.

"A woman was assaulted last week in Key West. A few days later, another woman was assaulted a few miles north. A couple of days after that, another one another few miles north of that one. If the timeline remains the same, whoever attacked these women could possibly be in our area either today or tomorrow."

Dmitry growled. "And you let me leave my mate at home, alone?"

"He's only attacked sex workers so far. Still, I hear you. I'm not any happier leaving Hannah by herself right now." Serge sighed. "I'd like to send Hannah, Kerrigan, and Megan on a trip for a couple of days, but I seriously doubt—"

Roman laughed. "Not going to happen. Megan's way too stubborn to be 'sent away'."

I shrugged into a t-shirt and watched as the three mated members of the team fretted over their mates' safety. I was lucky that I didn't have to worry. Of course, I wanted a mate, but at least without one I was spared going into freak-out mode every time the slightest hint of danger arose. Having a mate appeared to turn an otherwise level-headed bear into a crackpot. Going solo, at least I didn't have to worry about my blood pressure.

As the conversation turned into a discussion about how to protect one's mate without her detection, I looked over at Maxim. "Are we needed here?"

He snorted. "Not for this part."

Konstantin looked over at us and frowned. "Mate or not, we should all be concerned about the women on the island."

I sighed. "If you don't lighten up, you're headed for a stroke, Kon. You're way too high strung."

He just frowned deeper and turned back to Serge.

"Keep an ear out today, and your eyes open. Report anything out of the ordinary, asap." Serge sighed. "No one has been able to provide a description, so we're flying blind in that regard."

I got up and nodded to Serge. "Will do."

I left the office and headed down Main Street, using my keen shifter senses to astutely case the surrounding neighborhoods. I tended to be light-hearted, a jokester, but I took the job seriously. If there was someone on Sunkissed Key that was out to hurt women, I'd take him out and have absolutely no qualms about it. I may not have had a mate of my own, but I was fond of my team members' mates and I'd be damned if I'd let anything happen to them.

I wasn't halfway down Dolphin Avenue when I saw a man leading a woman away from the street. Something wasn't right about the scene. She looked as though she was with him willingly, but I scented an eagerness from him—and eagerness tinged with an evil, deranged enthusiasm. I followed. By the time I got to the rear of the house he'd led her behind, he'd already slipped a cloth over the woman's face and she was slumped against his body. Chloroform.

Beady eyes looked up at me from a hard face, and he bared his teeth. "What the fuck are you looking at?"

I tipped my head from side to side, popping my neck. "A dead man."

I reached out to the P.O.L.A.R. unit:

If you want this asshole to live, you'd better get here quick. I smiled outwardly. *Feel free to take your time.*

3

HEIDI

"Four Buds and six tequila shots!" Sarah hung half her body over the bar to call out the order to me. "In a rush!"

I popped the top of four ice cold bottles and slid them down to her. Making quick work of the shots, I slid them down, too, before tending to my customers seated at the bar. A handful of orders later and I finally got to slow down a bit. I took orders from the bar and doled out drinks as fast as I could. I was a damn good bartender. I'd done it for fun when I was barely old enough to see over the bar top and I hadn't really ever stopped.

My Uncle Joey owned a bar up in my hometown of Rocky Gorge, Colorado, and I'd ended up there every day after school from kindergarten through my senior year of high school. My parents, both high-powered career people, had been busy at work so Uncle Joey was the only one who could keep me. He'd taught me everything he knew, and by the time I was eleven, I could sling drinks like the finest Manhattan mixologists and put on a darn good show while doing it.

I put myself through a few years of college by bartending and when everything else in my life went to shit, bartending put a roof over my head and paid the bills. So, there I was, at the age of thirty, with nothing to show for my years of existence but a bunch of trick pours and head full of fancy cocktail recipes. Almost thirty, anyway. That next birthday was coming up faster than I liked.

"Heidi! I've got a big party that just got seated. You going to be ready for it, or should I tell Mimi to come out front and give you a hand?" My boss, and the owner of Mimi's Cabana, Mimi Tuatagaloa, was a plus sized Samoan woman who wore a coconut bra and grass skirt to work daily. Fortunately, she didn't make her employees do the same. Everyone loved Mimi, who was almost never without a smile. And, although she had curves on top of curves, she actually rocked the coconut bra thingy.

"No, I'm ready."

She looked at me and made a face.

I walked down to her. "What's up?"

"That table of fifteen. It's a table full of women on the island for a bachelorette party. You know that they're going to get hammered, fuck up their table, and forget to tip."

I winced. Bachelorette parties were notorious for being nothing but trouble for the waitresses. I felt for Sarah. "I'll share tips with you. Don't worry about that part."

She pouted. "You're the best, but you don't have to do that."

"It's not a problem. Come on. We'll start them off with a complimentary jello shot and maybe they'll be warmed up to you enough to remember to tip." I reached under the bar for the shots I'd made earlier in the day. Pulling a stack from the fridge, I slipped them onto Sarah's tray and winked. "No one needs to know that they're mostly jello."

She laughed and squeezed my hand before scooting away. I heard their rambunctious cheers just a few moments later. I hoped that they'd be a good group for her if they felt like she was being really cool to them.

When she came back a few minutes later with their drink orders, I just put my head down and got to work. Fifteen mojitos later, I was annoyed with muddling fresh mint and starting to get behind on the orders of the customers sitting at the bar, but I worked hard to get caught up.

Not even two minutes later, Sarah came back with one of the mojitos, frowning. "One of them doesn't like it."

I stiffened, but made another. When she came back right away, I frowned. "What is her deal? It's a mojito. What exactly is she looking for?"

Sarah looked worried. "She said she'd prefer it wasn't you who made her drink."

I felt my eyebrows try to crawl off of my forehead. "Excuse me?"

"I'm sorry, Heidi. I think we're going to need to get Mimi out here. She's causing a fuss...because of you know what."

My stomach sank and embarrassment rose. I kept my face expressionless, though. I wasn't going to show that it got to me. "Think I should just go talk to her?"

Sarah shook her head. "No, I don't think this is one of those situations that can be made better. I think she was a huge Callie super fan."

I tipped my head back and stared up at the ceiling of the bar. Toothpicks with little ribbons of color had been shot into the tiles up there over the years and it was hard to find a spot of ceiling that wasn't dotted with color. My past was colorful as well, to say the least. The fact that it'd been almost eight years and I was still getting negative reactions was insane, though. The whole thing should have been long forgotten by now. It certainly wasn't, though. Not by some people.

"Okay. Call Mimi up front. Have her make the damned mojito. I'll take care of the rest of them, if that's okay."

"I'm sorry, Heidi."

I shrugged and focused on the patrons at the bar. I poured drinks and took care of them as fast as I could while still plastering a smile on my face. It wasn't easy.

Hours passed and as the bar thinned out, the bachelorette party remained. They'd had plenty to drink and eat, but didn't look as though they planned to move their party elsewhere. Mimi was still interrupting her paper work in the back office to come up front and make the brat's drinks, since the woman was adamant that I not taint anything of hers with my unholy touch. Mimi should've been able to leave earlier in the night, and let Sarah and me close, but she stayed because of the brat.

I was discouraged and angry, but there was nothing I could do about it. I just had to take it. I wasn't going to chance making Mimi or her bar look bad. Mimi's Cabana was a Polynesian themed tiki bar that Mimi herself had opened almost twenty years ago. I was going to smile and carry on like nothing bothered me. Just ignore the hater.

That had been the plan, anyway, except the brat got emboldened by her Mimi-made mojitos and approached the bar. My smile was brittle and I wanted to excuse myself, but that never shut people up. The best thing, or so I'd discovered, was to face the hate head on and simply smile through it.

Brat floated over to me immersed in a cloud of Chanel, alcohol, and cigarette smoke. Her blonde hair was spiral curled and her eyes were smoked out perfectly. She was beautiful, all except the dark scowl on her face. "I know who you are."

I winced at the way she said it. It wasn't just a statement; it was an accusation. I held my smile firmly in place and rested my hands on the bar. I noticed that my nails were chipped beyond belief and pulled them back to my sides. "Heidi Garcia."

She scowled harder, her lip tucked up into a sneer Elvis would've been proud of. "Homewrecking Heidi. The Cuban slut of the decade, Heidi."

I shrugged it off. "If you're dead set on believing everything you see on TV, that's your problem. The bar is closing in half an hour. Do you need anything before it does?"

"Not from the likes of you. Who knows where your hands have been?" She flipped her hair over her shoulder and shook her head. "How you even show your face in public is beyond me."

4

ALEXEI

The sun was just breaching the horizon when I slipped into the ocean that morning. It was earlier than I normally went for a swim, but I'd had a restless night after disposing of the asshole who'd been preying on women around the Keys. My animal never felt guilty for what the job sometimes entailed. To him, it was clear cut. But it just sat a little heavier with my human side.

The water was cooler than normal and I took my time gliding through it, letting it wash my cares away. I swam out farther than I normally had time to and watched as a cruise ship powered by. Cruise ships didn't make a lot of sense to me. I didn't get the idea of locking yourself away in a small room, or set of rooms and calling it a vacation. Why go out onto the ocean for that? You could do that on land. I'd rather just swim in the water, like I was.

When the sun was cresting over the houses on the east side of the island, I swam closer to shore and floated on my back. The waves rocked me soothingly and I considered taking a nap. My bear loved naps. As I was contemplating it, a scent wafted through the air around me and captured my attention fully.

I looked around for the source and spotted an unfamiliar woman on the pier. She was too far for me to make out much about her, but I could smell her just fine. The wind was carrying her delicious aroma directly to me. She scented of vanilla and something sweet and sugary that reminded me of freshly glazed donuts, my absolute weakness. Completely entranced, I swam closer.

The woman sat on the end of the pier, facing the ocean, a fishing pole in one hand, a cup of coffee in the other. Her tall, statuesque body, from what I could tell, was a work of art, curving out and dipping in and so many fun places. In short cut off denim shorts and a cut off t-shirt, she was incredible. Her bare toes were painted a bright blue and my tongue lolled out, wanting to lick every part of her.

The face of an angel, she stared out at the ocean pensively, her eyes narrowed in concentration. I wondered what she was thinking.

Her line caught and she jumped into action, reeling in whatever was tugging on the end of it. She fought hard but after about a minute of wrestling with it, the line snapped and she fell back on her ass. Instead of cursing or getting angry, she knelt and patiently repaired her broken line and then cast it again. Her face remained serene the entire time, like she couldn't possibly have been doing anything more relaxing.

I wanted to sit on the pier with her. I swam closer, my bear drawn magnetically to her. There was something about her that just called to the both of us.

When I was close enough to see the bright green of her eyes, I bobbed in the water under the pier, wondering what I should do next. I wanted to interact with her. My bear wanted to play. I contemplated for a few more minutes and then swam out from under the pier. Looking up at her, waiting for her to see me, I chuffed in annoyance when she didn't.

She was so focused on whatever thoughts were buzzing around her head, she didn't notice me. I chuffed again and splashed a little water at her feet. Still nothing. I was a huge fucking polar bear in a tropical setting and she wasn't noticing me. What the hell?

Feeling more determined, I splashed a little harder. When that didn't work, I grabbed her fishing line and yanked on it.

She snapped to attention and looked down, her hand already reeling in the line. Her eyes moved right past me at first. I was about to become highly offended when they snapped back to me with a laser focus, and she let out a squeal that just about popped my eardrums. Stumbling backwards, she fell on her ass again and crab walked nearly halfway back up the pier, towards land.

I took her forgotten pole into my mouth and swam towards her. I hadn't meant to scare her. My bad. I should've thought through how anyone might react to seeing a big ass polar bear in the water next to them. We didn't exactly have a reputation for being gentle and cuddly.

I pawed at the water and tried to grin at her, but it must've looked more like a snarl because she blanched and yanked herself up by the wooden post between us. She stared down at me, those green eyes wide with fear. Her mouth worked up and down. Her pink tongue slipped out to wet her lips, and then vanished into her mouth again.

Just that flash of tongue sent a rocket of heat pulsing through me that rivaled even the hottest Florida sunshine. I wanted to climb the pier and beg her to do it again. As a man. The bear would have to kick rocks for a while.

She leaned over the railing and blinked. "You can't be real."

I chuffed and splashed her with a swipe of my paw. Her shorts grew darker and I watched droplets of water roll down her long, tan legs. I was real, alright.

Her hands went to her hips and she narrowed her eyes at me. "Okay, so maybe you are real."

I chuffed louder and splashed her again. I was having fun. I also selfishly wanted the t-shirt she was wearing to cling a little more tightly to her curves.

She slowly moved towards the beach a few steps and paused when I followed her. "Please don't eat me," she whispered. "I promise I won't taste good."

I flashed her my teeth again because I was pretty sure she'd taste delicious—better than anything I'd ever tasted before in my life.

She walked a little faster towards the beach and then broke into an outright run when she saw I was still following her. She was fast, but I was much faster. I got to the beach before her and tore across the sand so I could meet her at the mouth of the pier.

Panting, she froze when she saw that I was blocking her path. She looked scared, but the set of her jaw spoke of a stubborn resolve. I worried about that, because it looked like she was willing to go head to head with a polar bear. This particular situation aside, that would be very unwise. "You are *not* going to eat me, big fella. Do you hear me? I've got shit to do today."

I didn't want to scare her. My bear balked at the idea. He flopped down in front of her, rolled onto his back, and looked up at her like some docile puppy. I was nearly a thousand pound animal, but it seemed that I was putty in her hands. I spit her pole out at her feet and gave her my best "sweet and innocent" look.

"What the hell was my coffee spiked with?" She rubbed at her eyes and shook her head. When she looked at me again, she took a deep breath and reached a shaking hand out to touch me. Her fingers brushed my fur and she yelped again.

I sat up and gave her a look that I hoped implied that I didn't love her screaming at me, but that I wouldn't hurt her.

She held up her hands and let out a shaky laugh. "Sorry, sorry. I wasn't sure you were real. You are, though. You're very much real. Jesus H Christ. What is a polar bear doing in the waters off the Florida Keys? What are you doing here, big guy?"

She smelled better up close. I couldn't stop myself from leaning into her and nuzzling my head into her chest. She was silky soft. My nose ended up caught in the heavenly valley between her breasts. I sniffed her again and again, trying to imprint that delicious aroma on my brain.

She stood frozen, her hands held out to the sides of me in obvious fear. When I moved and rubbed my head against her hand, she let out another squeak and jostled backwards. I was desperate for her to touch me at that point, so I followed and rubbed against her again.

"Please don't eat me. Please." She muttered the words before turning her hand over and lightly resting it on my head.

Heaven.

5

HEIDI

I was touching a polar bear. There was a real, live polar bear right here in Sunkissed Key and I was touching it and I was probably going to die a gruesome death as its morning snack. My fear subsided ever so slightly as the giant animal blinked and rubbed its muzzle against me. It was heavy and the weight of it knocked me back a step. Every time I moved, it followed, though. I wasn't sure if I wanted to cry or laugh. I had to be dreaming.

It buried its nose between my breasts again and huffed. It seemed to like putting its nose there, but I was terrified it was going to bite off something that I couldn't easily replace.

"Please be careful. I want to keep both of those."

The giant bear chuffed at me, a noise that sounded oddly like a chuckle, and then lifted its head and ran its large, black tongue over my face. I stepped back, shocked by the gesture.

It sat back on its haunches again and seemed to smile at me. It even lifted its hand in what looked to be a wave. I just stared. I couldn't be seeing what I thought I was seeing. No way.

When it waved again, it smiled even larger and then chuffed again. If I didn't know better, I would've thought it was laughing at me.

I looked around, waiting on someone to pop out and yell, "Surprise," or, "You just got punked," or "You're on Candid Camera." Only, no one did. It was early in the morning, the sun had barely risen, and the beach was deserted. The sound of seagulls was the only thing that could be heard, other than my heavy breathing and the polar bear's, uh, laughter...?

"What the actual fuck?" I rubbed at my eyes, but quickly had to drop my hands again to keep from falling over as the giant animal bumped its nose into my stomach. "This isn't real. This *can't* be real. Polar bears don't live on Sunkissed Key. Polar bears don't swim up to the beach and rub up against people."

He sat up again and, I swear to god, blew me a kiss.

"Okay, now I know my coffee was spiked with a hallucinogen." I moved in closer, feeling emboldened by the idea that it was probably just a big dog—a Great Pyrenees, maybe. Or, it was a wealthy woman in a white fur coat. Although, why wouldn't someone wear a fur coat on the beach? *Wait, no, don't ask that. No trying to make rationalizations while your brain is on LSD, Heidi.*

I ran my fingers over its chest, and they got lost in its thick fur. I surreptitiously searched for a seam because maybe it was a costume, and—

"Eek!" I was suddenly plastered against the bear's stomach as it wrapped its massive paws around me.

Holy shit! Struggling to get my footing back, I ran my hands up to its face, assuming I'd be able to remove the mask. What I found instead were the sharpest set of teeth I'd ever felt. A wet mouth, sharp teeth, and a wide tongue that was rough as it stroked itself over my hand. The tip of one of those teeth pricked my finger and I gasped before yanking my hand away.

Real polar bear. I was in the arms of a real fucking polar bear. I froze in fear, thinking I was about to die. No matter what happened next, I was a dead woman. I could feel the massive paws of the thing trapping me against it, its body heat scalding me, and the weight of it as it rested its chin on the top of my head. I wanted to scream, but I didn't think it would help anything, besides, it might rile the creature and hasten my demise.

It was too late for me.

I was a goner.

"D-do you think you can make it quick?" I buried my fingers in its fur and turned my head so I wasn't being suffocated. My cheek was pressed against its chest, its growling vibrating me. "Please, kill me fast. I don't want it to be like those nature shows, where you eat my leg and I live for another two days until you come back to gnaw on my arms. Just...go for the head first, okay?"

The thing chuffed again and then released me. It looked down at me and I swear it rolled its eyes. Then, it went down on all fours and started rubbing against me again.

"So...does this mean you're not gonna eat me, then?"

Its tongue came out and stroked over my stomach. Then, the tip of its nose dug under my shirt and I had to step away and push my shirt down to keep from being exposed.

If I didn't know better, I would've said that bear had been around too many human men in its life. It seemed...tame, though. It didn't seem to want to hurt me. The whole thing just got weirder and weirder.

Like a lightbulb, I suddenly remembered the animal sanctuary on the island. The Sunkissed Wildlife Sanctuary was a tourist attraction for the island. The man who ran the place took in animals that had been retired from Hollywood, or traveling circuses. I'd never been, because the idea of it made me sad for the poor animals, but evidently my polar bear was from there. Mr. (Leon) Zoo, a surname legalized through a "Florida Petition for Change of Name" form and a filing fee, ran the place. I'd bet money he was probably frantically searching one large, displaced polar bear.

"You're from the animal sanctuary, aren't you, big fella?" Knowing the animal was probably retired from some weird circus made me feel slightly better. He was probably old and lost, but used to humans. That was why he hadn't eaten me. Yet. "You want to go back home? I'm sure Mr. Zoo is missing you right now. He probably hates the thought of having to send out a missing polar bear alert to the local authorities."

The bear licked my stomach again and then my face. Then, he rested his chin on my shoulder and made a happy, almost purring sound.

"You're not so scary." I swallowed. "Well, okay, that's a lie. You are scary, but you're sweet, too."

I looked up him and wondered how I could lead a bear back to the sanctuary. It wasn't as though I had a leash or anything. The back entrance to the place wasn't all that far. Maybe I could actually cut behind my house and across Pelican Drive to get him back home. I didn't know how to get a bear to follow me, though. Too bad I hadn't caught my fish of the day or I'd use that to lure him. Not that I especially wanted to dangle a snack in my hand and tease a half-ton apex predator with it.

"If I lead the way, will you follow me?" I edged away from him and moved back to the beach. He'd pushed me back onto the pier, slowly but surely, and I was starting to worry about it being on the old wooden structure with such a large animal. "Come on. I bet Mr. Zoo is really worried that you're out here, getting yourself into trouble."

Miraculously, he just followed me. Without hesitation, he walked along right behind me as I headed toward the sanctuary. It was crazy, but then again, not crazier than anything else that had happened in the past ten minutes. All the way past my house and in between two houses on Pelican Drive, we went. I crossed my fingers that no one came out and had a stroke over the sight. Then, when we reached the back entrance of the wildlife sanctuary, Mr. Zoo seemed to have anticipated our arrival.

I was about to knock on the wooden gate when it swung open. He took one look at my polar bear and sighed loudly. I smiled, as best as I could in my still slightly apprehensive state. "Did you lose something?"

He reached out and patted the bear on the nose and nodded. "Thanks for bringing him back. He's a major troublemaker, but harmless as a pussycat."

I shrugged, like it was no big deal and I hadn't been so terrified a few minutes ago that I'd begged the polar bear to eat my head first. "He's really cuddly."

"Oh, I'm sure he is that." He maneuvered around the bear and shifted his weight into pushing the ass end of the bear inside the gate. "Thanks, again."

I watched as he led the creature away and felt oddly sad when the gate closed and I was separated from my bear. *The* bear, not *my* bear. Why did I think of him as mine?

6

ALEXEI

I shifted back to my human self and glared at the zookeeper, who was a shifter himself. Some sort of buffalo, if my sense of smell wasn't mistaken. Leon Zoo, a man the team had lectured a few times regarding the way he kept his animals, was a jackass. "I should bite your head right off your shoulders for prodding me in the ass like that."

"Oh, excuse me. I'm not really up on the normal protocol for herding a *shifter* into my compound. Not to mention having to pretend that I just *lost* an animal—a polar bear no less! I have a reputation, you know."

I rolled my eyes. "Not a very good one."

"You can leave now, sunshine."

I left, naked, and snuck back to the pier to find my shorts. Then, after looking around and having no luck spotting my human, went back to the house. My bear was damn near giddy with excitement at the morning's events. I thought of the way he'd rubbed himself all over her and laughed. Maybe that hadn't been all him.

I should've felt bad for the way I'd touched her and tasted her skin, but she was utterly irresistible. I was aroused just thinking about the way she'd felt as her fingers stroked my fur. I wanted to feel her against my human body. I wanted more than to feel her.

I let myself into the house and went straight to the kitchen. I was famished. If I couldn't have her right then, I was going to need to satisfy myself in other ways. Luckily for me, Serge was there, cooking.

"Thank god. I was afraid I was going to have to cook for myself."

Serge looked me over and raised his eyebrows. "You look keyed up. What's up?"

I couldn't tell him the truth. We weren't supposed to interact with humans in our animal form the way I just had. Not without a good enough reason. Serge wouldn't consider just wanting to be close to her a good enough reason. "Just had a refreshing swim."

He made a face. "Uh huh."

I watched and as soon as he put the first stack of pancakes on the island, I grabbed them. He complained, but I didn't care. I poured a half a bottle of syrup over them and dove in head first. I didn't come up until the ache in my stomach eased up some and I felt the beginnings of a sugar coma. It was easier in that state to not be so focused on my new human obsession.

"What the hell, Alexei?"

I grinned and pushed away from the counter. "Thanks. I'm heading up to get ready for work."

"Asshole."

I waved Serge off and took the stairs up to my room, three at a time. I grabbed a towel and a change of clothes before stepping into the bathroom. What started out as an innocent shower soon became my hand wrapped around my cock, the woman from the pier's tall, sexy body playing across my mind until I came with a low growl.

I had to see her again. I didn't know what it was about her, but I was smitten. I not only wanted to see her and touch her more, I *needed* to, as crazy as that was.

The rest of the day passed in a blur. We had a steady stream of asinine jobs, with Halloween right around the corner. It seemed everyone got a little wilder around that time—shifter and human alike. All day, I went through the motions, but I was distracted as hell.

It was early when I fell into bed, and I laid there counting down the hours until I could go back to that pier. I hoped she'd come back there. She *had* to. I'd never seen her around the island before, but surely she wasn't a tourist. She was out fishing, and by herself. That wasn't touristy activity.

By the time morning came, I was climbing out of my skin, eager to find her again. It was still dark when I left the house and sank into the ocean. Hooking my shorts where I always left them, I shifted and swam out to sea, using the time to swim hard and really push my bear. He needed to work on releasing some energy before seeing our little human. It would be too easy to get overly excited and accidentally hurt her.

Again, as the sun was coming up on the east side of the island, turning the horizon a deep purple color, I swam up closer to the pier and watched as she appeared. Strolling down the beach then stepping onto the pier, the slight sway of her hips was hypnotizing. She was all long legs and perfect curves and her bare feet made the softest of sounds as she stepped. She stopped at the end of the pier and pulled her fishing pole out before hesitating and scanning the water.

If I wasn't mistaken...hmm...was there hope in her eyes as she looked around? Then she spotted me. The corners of her lips lifted as she braced herself on the railing and leaned forward.

"What are you doing out, again?" She watched me swim closer and giggled when I splashed water at her again. "You're a naughty boy, aren't you?"

Naughty? She had no clue. I swam closer and then ducked under the water right in front of her. Swimming as deep as I could and then shooting back up, I did my version of a bear grin when she squeaked and pursed her lips. I belly flopped back into the water and my large splash soaked her.

Her caramel colored hair clung to her head and face and the tie-dye shirt she wore suctioned to her breasts. "You're a ham. Come on. Let's get you back to Mr. Zoo. As rude as he may be, that's where you belong."

I growled and splashed her again. I wasn't done hanging out with her. I went under again and found a large fish. I easily caught it and came up with it between my teeth. Getting as close to her as I could, I spit it out next to her feet on the pier and tried to grin again. Damn, I wanted to be in my human form.

She squatted, giving me a glorious view of her inner thighs, and picked it up. "Is this for me?"

I nodded my head and then swam alongside the pier, needing to be closer to her. She grabbed her things and followed me, the fish tucked into the bucket she'd carried up. She hurried along with an excited expression. It seemed that she was as eager as I was.

When we both got to the beach, I made myself slow down so I didn't hurt her. Her fear from yesterday seemed to have vanished. She came right up to me and stroked my head. When I purred like a fucking kitten, she leaned into me and scratched me with both hands.

"You're a real charmer, aren't you?"

I ran my tongue over her neck and let out a low growl. That spot... I wanted to bury my face there and taste her for weeks. Or months. I wasn't sure which.

She shivered against me and I eased up my affections. I let her touch me more, let her stroke my fur and scratch me behind the ears like I was a dog. It should've been embarrassing, but it wasn't. I was in heaven and wanting more of her touch.

I wanted to shift and show her how much I really liked what she was doing. I wanted to strip her naked and worship at the temple of her body. I wasn't fool enough to think that she wouldn't run screaming if I suddenly shifted and became a man in her arms, though.

7

HEIDI

"You know that this is crazy, right? You're a polar bear. You're not supposed to be out just roaming a Florida beach by yourself. You know? Mr. Zoo should really keep better tabs on you." I hugged my new favorite animal again and then pulled away. "You're such a snuggle bear. I can't stop hugging you."

He used a big paw to draw me back closer to him and made a happy little noise when I fell against him. He'd seemed as excited to see me as I'd been to see him and I hadn't felt an ounce of fear that morning. I'd *wanted* to find him. It made no sense, but there it was. I supposed that after the first encounter, my sixth sense kicked in and now I viewed him as completely harmless which was really stupid considering the fact that no matter how tamed he'd been by the circus or trainer or whoever had him before Mr. Zoo, he was a wild and potentially deadly animal. Still, I'd never even known a dog that was as lovable and cuddly as he was.

"Come on. As much as I'd love to take you home and let you live with me, I'm sure that would violate about fifty local ordinances. You have to go back to Mr. Zoo." I sighed. "Maybe this time he'll do a better job at containing you so you can't get out again."

Again, same as yesterday, I led him back to the sanctuary and knocked on the gate. I looked back at him and sighed again. He kept staring at me with his eyes all big and pleading, like he wanted something from me. He seemed to be attracted to me and I wanted to spend the rest of the day hanging out with him. That wasn't the adult in me speaking, though. No way should a polar bear be on this island unless it was in a cage or reinforced enclosure of some sort. I couldn't keep him out in public, where something could set him off. At the end of the day, he was a wild animal.

It was hard to believe he was a wild animal when I looked at him, though. "You're too darn cute, you know that?"

Mr. Zoo opened the gate when my bear chuffed out what I thought of as a laugh. He took one look at us and rolled his eyes—not the reaction I was anticipating—before gesturing the bear inside. The bear was obviously well trained in non-verbal commands because Mr. Zoo didn't say a word the whole time. The bear just lumbered in and Mr. Zoo closed the gate after him.

I stood there, feeling angry and lonely, all of a sudden. I wanted to go in with my bear and make sure he was being cared for. I didn't get the impression that that would be a welcome intrusion, though. So, instead, I forced myself to walk back to the beach.

It made no sense to feel sad and lonely after returning a stray animal to his proper home. So why, I pondered as I gathered my fishing supplies, did I suddenly feel hollow inside? It was the strangest thing. I almost felt as though I'd had to give away a pet dog that had been my loyal companion for years.

It was also foreign for me to feel lonely. I'd gotten used to the solitary life that I'd built for myself. I hadn't felt lonely in years. Yet, the hollow pit inside begged to differ.

At home, I put my supplies away and carried my fish—the gift from my polar bear—inside. It was a nice looking fish and larger than the fish I usually caught. I put it on ice. It would make a delicious dinner later. A fish caught by a polar bear. I shook my head at the very thought and went to shower and get ready to head over to Maria's to watch the boys.

My morning with Jayden and Jonas was spent fending off their cuteness attacks and taking them out to play on the beach. By the time Maria got home from work, I had lunch prepared for her. I said my goodbyes and see ya' tomorrows and left to slip back home and take care of some errands before heading to work at the bar that night.

I was in the middle of my errands when I ran into *him*. At the grocery store, heading up the canned good aisle, *he* stepped into the aisle and walked towards me.

Tall, broad, sexier than hell. He was a muscled god in a tight-fitting t-shirt and camo pants. Army camo, I noticed right away. His blonde hair was sun-bleached and kind of went everywhere all at once, a little too long. I had the strangest urge to run my hands through that hair.

I'd never felt such an instant attraction before. It was like someone had suddenly turned the heat up in the canned goods aisle. I was instantly aware that I hadn't changed out of the thin tank top I'd worn to play with the boys earlier. I felt on display and the way *his* eyes raked over my body told me very clearly that I was.

I'd never seen him before, but I instantly had an idea of who he was. I'd heard plenty of talk at the bar about the group of military looking guys who'd moved onto the island several months back. A few of them had even stopped into Mimi's on occasion—not this one, though. Apparently, they all lived in a large house that used to be a B&B, and rented office space on Main Street. No one knew what exactly they did or why they were here, but looks-wise, they had the locals in a tizzy. The women, anyway. Some men, too. Seeing *him*, I now understood why.

His cart was empty when he parked it next to me. I averted my eyes and pretended to be highly interested in a can of beets. I went as far as to twist the can so I could read the label. Yep, still beets.

As he reached over me to grab a can of sauerkraut, his arm just barely grazed my shoulder when he pulled back. "Oh, sorry."

My skin burned and tingled where he'd touched me and I had to work to make my mouth form words to respond. "No problem."

He dropped the can in his cart and stepped back just slightly. "I'm Alexei. I don't think I've seen you around the island before."

I looked up at him and took a deep breath. He was so tall—6'4" or 6'5". At 5'11", I wasn't a short woman by any means, taller than average, but he was a giant. His eyes...they were crystal blue like tropical waters. His eyelashes, long and thick, made those eyes look bedroom ready.

"Um... Heidi."

The corner of his lips raised in a sexy half-smile for a split second before repeating my name. He said it with his deep voice and just the slightest bit of an accent. "Are you new to the island?

I realized I still had my hand lifted in mid-air, halfway to the can of beets, and immediately dropped it. "No, actually. I've lived here for a number of years."

He reached up to grab another can from behind me, and his chest came even closer to me. He smelled...familiar. I couldn't place it, but it was a scent that made me happy, like ocean and sun. I wanted to breathe him in deeper, maybe even bury my face in that broad chest to get more of it. I almost asked what kind of cologne he used.

When he pulled back, his jaw muscles worked. "Has anyone ever told you that you smell like fresh glazed donuts?"

I laughed. "Like donuts? No, nope. I can't say I've heard that before."

He dropped another can into his cart and smiled down at me. His teeth were perfect, of course, and when he exposed them, I felt like he was more animal than man. That smile held a hint of a warning and an overwhelming sex appeal. Until he spoke again. "You know, if you asked me out, I wouldn't say no."

Hold the brakes! Cute, sexy, but cocky and arrogant as hell. Dangerous, too. I wasn't going to take that warning lightly. He was too much man, too much heat and promise. My body wanted to adhere to him like a suction cup. My stomach was a flutter of butterflies, all beating wings toward him. I wasn't stupid, though. I knew trouble when I saw it.

"Enjoy your sauerkraut." I forced myself to grab my cart and step away from him.

Walking away from him felt like trudging through quick dry concrete. My body begged for a chance to rub against that big, delicious hunk of a man. I'd been so long since I'd been with anyone, but Alexei wasn't a man to fan some flames with. He was all inferno and I already had metaphorical burn scars. I'd vowed never again. So, as hard as it was to fight the pull, I kept walking, headed to the checkout, unwilling to run into him again. I wasn't sure I'd be as strong a second time.

8

ALEXEI

I showed up the next morning with a wounded ego and a desperation to see Heidi. I'd spent the previous night at Cap'n Jim's Bar and Grill, drinking and licking my wounds. I had felt a wild attraction to Heidi as soon as I saw her, but seeing her while not in bear form, while I could talk to her and get skin to skin with her was an entirely different thing.

As soon as I'd seen her in that tiny tank top, her long, flat torso exposed, I'd wanted to rip it off of her, while simultaneously needing to cover her from anyone else looking her way. She was tall and slender but curvy in the right places and had the most exotically beautiful coloring—skin and hair the color of caramel and light green eyes with a darker green ring around the iris.

I'd been so sure that she'd felt the same attraction. I'd seen the way she looked at me. Yet, maybe I'd been mistaken.

The memory of how easily she'd brushed me off compounded the discomfort of my melancholy and my hangover that morning. Still, I floated next to the pier, waiting for her to show up. And she did! The moment I saw her, a desperate neediness and longing arose in me and I knew I looked like one of those fucking animal rescue commercials.

Heidi didn't saunter her way down the pier like she normally did. She stopped on the beach and slid her little jean shorts down her hips. Her tank top followed and then she waded into the water in a small yellow bikini that left me drooling.

I swam closer to her, ready to rub all over her, but she beat me to it. When she was close enough, she wrapped her arms around my neck and hugged me.

"You big devil. How the heck did you get out again? If I didn't think you were completely harmless and didn't love to see you so much, I'd report Mr. Zoo to the authorities. Or, are you some kind of Houdini of the animal kingdom?" She moved back and scratched the top of my nose. "Come on. Let's have a swim before I have to take you back to that sorry excuse for a zookeeper."

I wanted to stay distant, but my bear wasn't having it. He was overjoyed at having her next to him, splashing us back. She swam beautifully, in long strokes that cut through the water easily. When she was far enough, I nudged her with my nose, worried about her going too far out. I wouldn't let anything happen to her, but still, I worried.

As she swam in place, she chatted away. Her mood was bright that morning, her eyes glittering as she looked at me. She spoke to me like I was a pet. Or a friend, not just some random animal, and I found myself listening to everything she said with apt attention. I wanted to know more. Maybe she wanted nothing to do with me as a man, but I could still spend time with her.

After a few more minutes of swimming, she moved closer to the beach and stood in waist deep water, looking around. "This place is so beautiful. And you're displaced in this setting but I think that makes the fact that you're here even more extraordinary. I wish I had a camera right now."

When I grunted, she laughed.

"I swear you can understand me. It's amazing that I just went for a swim with a polar bear, but I feel like you're my buddy. And I should probably be checking myself into a mental health facility." She stroked my face and sighed. "If not for talking to polar bear like he's my long lost pet pooch, then for walking away from that hot guy in the grocery store yesterday."

I perked right up. I was afraid to move for fear of her changing the subject.

"*He* was beautiful. Sexy, muscled, he had literally everything going for him. He even smelled good. Too bad he was cocky as hell, although he had good reason to be, I'm sure." She tilted her head back to dip her hair into the water, giving me a full view of her chest. "I know I should be over an interaction that lasted all of two or three minutes, but I had a dream about him last night. I woke up in a hell of a state, all hot and sweaty. I still haven't been able to get him off my mind."

Unable to resist, I ran my tongue up her stomach. When she squealed and splashed me with water, I just grinned at her.

"Keep your tongue to yourself." She wagged her finger at me. "You have nothing to worry about. You're still the most interesting guy in my life. I walked away from Hottie McHotterson. I can spot trouble when I see it and he had trouble written all over him."

I wanted to tell her that I wasn't trouble. I was a good time.

"Although, you're trouble, too. You keep breaking out of the Wildlife Sanctuary and Mr. Zoo's going to find some other refuge to take you. You'll be too much of a risk." She frowned. "Does he treat you well?"

I desperately wanted to shift and talk to her. I wanted to tell her who I was and how I felt like we were buddies too and that I wouldn't be trouble. I'd take her out and I'd listen to her talk about whatever she wanted, like I was listening now.

She sighed and twisted her hair into a knot on top of her head. "I'm conversing with a polar bear like it's not utterly bizarre."

I grunted. It wasn't bizarre. She liked me. I liked her. She would like human me, too, if she'd give me a chance.

"Okay, my big snuggle bear, it's time to get you back to Mr. Zoo's." She held my head in her hands and brushed a kiss over my nose. "He told me I smelled like fresh doughnuts. Ugh! I'm thinking of him again! Okay, I'm stopping right now."

Following her back to Zoo's place was no fun. I didn't want our time to end and I especially didn't want to have to wait another day to see her again. I was hooked.

She stopped before she knocked on the door of the sanctuary and I mentally called out to Leon Zoo telling him not come to the gate yet. "I wish I could bring the boys to see you. Jayden and Jonas would flip out. Maria would have a heart attack. Rightfully so. I'm not ready to share our time together yet, though. Although, this will probably be the last time. Mr. Zoo's got to do something about you wandering around the island. I know you're a sweetheart, but still."

I pushed against her and nuzzled my face into her chest. I wanted to remain with her. For a second, I was starting to feel like I actually was an animal being dropped off at the zoo. I didn't want to be left behind. My bear was miserable, too. We were both desperate to stay with her.

She knocked on the gate and smiled at me, though. "Is it weird that I'll miss you? Yeah, it's weird. I probably need a lobotomy."

I grunted at her and then growled at Leon Zoo as he opened the gate and waved me in. Once again, I left Heidi's side and stepped into the sanctuary reluctantly. The gate shut and she was left on the other side.

I was spurred with a determination to see more of her, though. A few minutes in the mornings with her just wasn't enough.

9

HEIDI

That night at work, Hottie McHotterson, a.k.a. Alexei, showed up. He was with another guy, both of them in similar outfits of tight, black t-shirts and some type of canvas military pants. Heads turned and jaws dropped as the two of them walked in. Alexei had combed his hair back from his face and it looked like he'd been running his hands through it over and over again. It had the effect of making me want to run *my* hands through it.

I'd been mid-pour on a whiskey double when I spotted him. He wasn't reserved about his intention. He was staring right at me as though his eyes were laser pointers boring holes in me. His slow smirk heated my blood and he nodded to his friend before heading over to me. I wasn't able to take my eyes off of him until I felt liquid splashing on my hand and looked down to find I was still pouring the whiskey into an overflowing glass.

Cursing, I put my bottle down and slid the glass towards the customer, not caring that I'd given him more than he was paying for. I leaned towards Alexei and raised a brow. "Coincidence?"

He flashed those pearly whites and shook his head. "Not even close."

"Just stubborn then?"

He bit his lower lip and grunted. "You could say that."

I rested my hands on the bar in front of him. "What would you like to drink?"

"Whatever's on tap." He watched as I poured him a beer and brought it over to him. "You're a hard woman to track down."

My stomach fluttered and I was about to answer when Sarah called out an order. I held up a finger to Alexei and went to fill the drinks. I worked fast, but my hands were shaky. I could feel his eyes on me, taking in everything I did.

When I passed the drinks to Sarah, she grinned. "Looks like you've got an admirer."

I glanced back at Alexei and released a breathy little sigh. "So, I do."

"Well? Why are you still over here? Go, girl, get him."

I wanted to drag her back and use her as an excuse to keep my distance from Alexei. The man still spelled out trouble with a capital T. Sarah vanished on me, though, and I had no choice but to scoot back over to him. The bar wasn't busy enough that I couldn't stand and talk to him for a bit.

"Hi." Alexei leaned towards me, his dark eyes focused on mine. He gave me a slow smile that sent heat coursing through my body. "I should apologize."

I found myself leaning into him and braced myself on the bar top. "For?"

"For not being able to take a brush off when I get one." He took a long pull from his beer. "I should've gone to Capt'n Jim's where I usually drink and left you alone, but I was craving glazed donuts."

I laughed suddenly, unable to help myself. "Are you always so full of shit?"

He grinned and shrugged. "Pretty much. Are you still denying me the pleasure of taking you out?"

"I don't remember denying you that. I remember you telling me that I could take you out."

"You're right. May I have the pleasure of taking you out?"

I heard someone call out an order but held his gaze. "No."

He laughed and the sound sent warmth pooling in my lower belly. His eyes practically twinkled and he bit his lower lip. "You're busy. I'll ask again when you're free."

"The answer will still be no."

"We'll see."

I shook my head as I moved away to fill more orders. When I got back to him, he was still watching me, his eyes hyper-focused. I just leaned against the bar and raised a brow. I was playing with fire, but I felt like there was something drawing me to his side, like a crazy strong magnet.

"Change your mind yet?"

I ducked my head to hide a smile. "You're stubborn."

"I like to think of it as determined." He glanced over his shoulder and his face grew serious as his friend came up beside him. His friend said something quietly to him and then he stood up. Leaning over the bar, he slipped a couple of bills into my hand. The brush of his skin over mine was electric, but he just moved back and forced a smile. "Duty calls."

I wanted to tell him to come back. It was insane. I wanted to slip him my number and tell him to call me, visit me, *whatever* me. Instead, I shrugged. "Saved yourself the embarrassment of another denial."

He winked at me and then was gone.

I sagged against the bar, not exactly sure what to do with myself after being so amped up while Alexei was there. Fortunately, my duty called, too. People came and went at the bar and I kept busy until the closing.

I slept fitfully that night, dreams of Alexei taunting me the entire night through. In the dreams, I was with him and my polar bear, swimming in the ocean. I could feel the brush of his legs against mine under the water, the way he wrapped his big arms around me, and the way his fingers trailed over my face. Some of the dreams had been sweet, while others had been enough to leave me blushing when I remembered them the next morning. Dream Heidi was a kinky woman.

I was wired. Wired and tired. It was a vicious combination that made me cranky. It was almost enough to keep me in bed and persuade me to skip my morning fishing routine. Almost. I couldn't resist going out to the pier on the off chance that maybe my polar bear had outwitted Mr. Zoo again and found a way to get out. I just skipped bringing my fishing gear and went straight there.

Only, when I arrived, he wasn't there. I waited around for a while, a part of me hopeful, but he never showed. Which was a good thing, or so I tried to tell myself. it wasn't safe for a polar bear to be freely roaming an inhabited island. Still, my mood sank lower and lower with each passing moment. I didn't understand why I was so tied to seeing the damn bear, but I was. When the sun had fully risen and one by one, joggers and sunbathers showed up on the beach, I headed to the animal sanctuary. I knocked on the back gate for what felt like eternity before Mr. Zoo opened it.

"What?"

I frowned. "I guess the polar bear didn't escape today."

"No."

"Could I see him?"

"No."

I stammered. "What?"

He shook his head. "No. Not today."

I stepped back and stared in shock as he slammed the gate in my face. What the hell? I crossed my arms over my chest and walked away muttering to myself about how he should be a little more grateful to me for saving his ass and returning one of his runaway animals to him—not once, not twice but three times. I had half a mind to go back and tell him what I thought about that but I had to get to work and, really, what was the point?

I wondered how he managed to contain my bear. Maybe he'd reinforced whatever home the bear was living in. I'd definitely have to go by and check on him.

10

ALEXEI

I showed back up at Mimi's Cabana the next night, unable to stay away from Heidi. I hadn't been able to see her that morning and I was jonesing for some time with her. The job from the night before had run over. Two hundred miles north of the island, we'd ended up chasing a rogue shifter through swampland. By the time we got back home, it was late morning—too late to show up at the pier where Heidi fished.

I half worried that she wouldn't be at Mimi's. I needed to know the other places on the island she frequented so I could plan to "accidentally" run into her. I'd spent the day searching for her, but I'd had no luck. As soon as I got close to the bar, though, I could smell her. She was there.

When I entered the place, I spotted her and knew right away that something was off. She had a frown on her face as she spoke to someone at the bar. She turned away from them before I could zone in and hear what she was saying. There were dark circles under her eyes and she looked tired. I wanted to fix whatever was making her frown like that.

That thought struck me, the truth of it settling into my bones. I wanted to take care of her, to hold her and to do whatever I could to make her feel better. No matter what was wrong, or what it took to fix it.

She glanced up from the bar at that moment and spotted me. Something passed over her face and then the corners of her mouth tipped up slightly. Her smile made my heart melt. Surely, she knew what it did to me.

I crossed to the bar and slid onto a stool. I didn't pretend that I wasn't watching her as she moved around, waiting on other customers who'd been there before me. Her body swayed, the short dress she wore flitted around her thighs as she moved. It was tantalizing, wondering if I'd catch a glimpse of one more inch of thigh when she grabbed a bottle of liquor from the top shelf or bent to grab a bottle of beer from the cooler under the bar. The curves of her breasts had me leaning forward and holding my breath as she leaned across the bar to hand someone a drink.

Then, there was the way her eyes kept landing back on me. Every few seconds, she glanced my way, her head down, looking through her lashes. I could see the pulse at the base of her throat work, smell her sweet, sugary scent strengthening. As she danced around behind the bar, working fast and efficiently, I felt like I was back in the wild, honing in on prey. When she turned her back to me, I could see the way her body tightened, like she was aware of the precarious position she'd put herself. Her body recognized the apex predator in mine, and maybe even felt the desire I had to leap over the bar, drag her off with me and make her mine.

When Heidi did make her way over to me, her eyes seemed brighter. The frown from earlier was gone. "Should I be worried that you're stalking me?"

I nodded. "Very."

"At least you're honest." She pushed her hair behind her ears. "Beer?"

"I can't stay." No matter how much I wanted to. "I just figured I'd try again. I'm hoping I can wear you down eventually with my masculine good looks and endearing charm."

Someone called for a drink but her eyes were locked on mine.

The bright green looked almost glowing in the lighting over the bar. "How long can you hear 'no' before it just breaks that endearingly charming heart?"

I stood up and leaned across the bar. Not touching her, I spoke with my lips only a hair away from her ear. "More times than either of us want to count. Save yourself the trouble."

Her blood pumped faster, her heartrate sped. A barely audible little intake of breath was followed by the scent of her sexual arousal filling my senses. "I don't think there's anything about you that isn't trouble, Alexei."

Hearing my name on her lips just about killed me. I just barely brushed my mouth over her ear before pulling away and leaving her in her own space. I ran my hand through my hair, the interaction shaking me probably more than it did her. I clamped my teeth down on my lip to keep from begging her.

Another call came for more drinks, but Heidi just held my gaze and shivered. "Like I said. Trouble."

I watched the guy who'd been talking to her earlier snap his fingers to get her attention. She frowned. He was clearly a fucking asshole. Just when I had decided to not rip his fingers off, I heard him lean over to his friend and snort.

"Maybe they need to replace bimbo over there with someone who can actually tend bar."

I knew Heidi had heard it. Her eyes dimmed again and she shook her head. "Sorry, I've got to get back to work."

I forced a smile and casually stepped over to the guy. I rested my arm along his shoulder and applied just the slightest bit of pressure. My anger was like a living, breathing entity. "Hello, friend."

The guy looked up, and up, at me, his smirk dying. "Hey."

I squeezed his shoulder tighter. "So, I got the impression that you don't know this lovely woman's name. It's Heidi. I'm sure you didn't mean to actually call her something other than Heidi."

He shifted, uncomfortable with my clear aggression, but not wanting to lose face in front of his friends. "Dude, fuck off."

I growled and he jumped. "I've had a long day and you're starting to piss me off. Not good. I'd hate to lose control and snap your head off your scrawny little neck."

He winced at the pressure I was putting on his shoulder. "Whatever, man."

"What's her name?"

His friends were leaning away from him, leaving him to face the big, bad bear alone. "Heidi."

"Good!" I patted his shoulder harshly and stepped back. "There we go. That wasn't so hard."

His hand went to his shoulder and he scowled at me. "I didn't mean anything by it."

I pulled out my wallet and threw several bills on the counter. "Of course you didn't. Have another beer on me."

I walked back to the end of the bar, grinned and nodded a goodbye to Heidi before heading out. I really didn't want to leave, but I had to get back to work.

"Alexei."

I stopped and turned.

Heidi made a face at me. "It doesn't mean I'm going out with you, but thanks."

I laughed. "You're welcome."

Her mouth worked like she was fighting back a grin and then she lost. Her lips stretched wide and she rolled her eyes before turning away. "My answer's still no."

"Uh huh."

11

HEIDI

"He's beautiful." I ran my hand over my bear's head and sighed. "He's this perfect specimen of maleness and he's hitting on me. And he gives me this feeling... I can't even describe it. It's like I *want* to throw caution to the wind and just go crazy all over him."

Bear rested his head on my knee and grunted.

"I can't, though. That's just not my life. And he doesn't know the truth about me." I looked out at the ocean and watched as the waves rolled onto the shore. It was a red flag sort of day, dangerous water to swim in but still beautiful to look at. Clouds hung heavily in the sky, but it wasn't supposed to rain until later in the day.

The gloomy, overcast skies should've had me feeling moody, but I was on a high from being pursued by Alexei. He made me laugh and something about him was intoxicating.

"I'm lonely. I hate to admit it, and I really didn't realize it until just a day or two ago, but I am." Maybe I was moodier than I realized. "My life is so full. I have the boys and Maria. I have other friends... I have..."

He adjusted his head and growled.

"Yes, I have you. Kind of. As much as one can have a polar bear with escape artist tendencies." I scratched behind his ears and kissed the top of his head. "I don't want to feel lonely. I was fine before he came along."

I *had* been fine. It had been easy to accept the life I'd chosen for myself when there hadn't been anything working against it. Alexei was working against that life. It was hard to be okay with being alone when there was someone as magnetic as Alexei showering me with attention.

"I came here to be alone. Almost a decade ago. I came with the expectation that I'd find solitude. Not counting Maria and the boys. I was okay with it. More than okay, I was happy with it. It was better than the other options, honestly."

The sound of a car door shutting somewhere in the distance pulled me from my reverie. I shook my head and patted my bear on the head. Houdini, as I was calling him, understood. He stood up with a growl and butted into me with his nose before backing up and letting me stand.

"I hate having to take you back to that jerk. I hope he's nicer to you than he is to me." We walked down the beach and took the path we always did to get to the sanctuary. "Maybe I'll bring the kids to the wildlife sanctuary today. No, not today. I promised them I'd take them to Clotilde's for ice cream today, and it's supposed to rain. But soon. I'll bring them soon."

I knocked on the gate and as we waited, Houdini rubbed against me and snorted, his big dark eyes seeming to smile at me.

"I bet you'd like ice cream. You probably like anything having to do with ice. I'm not sure anyone could afford to keep you fed with ice cream, though. I've seen the way you eat fish."

Abruptly, Mr. Zoo opened the door and ushered Houdini in. Without a word, the gate slammed shut and I stood there, frowning at it.

I couldn't dwell on the rudeness for long, though. I had to get to the boys and so Maria wasn't late for work. I stopped by my house to change quickly and then ran to Maria's. When I walked in, she had a twin hanging from each arm, both of them crying.

"Thank god you're here. Take them, please." She passed Jonas to me and then Jayden. "I've got to stop and get gas. I'm going to be late."

The boys cried harder. I bounced them on my hips and made soothing noises. "Sorry I'm late, Maria. I got caught up."

"Doing whatever it is that's making your face light up lately but you won't tell me about?"

I snorted. "You'd better go."

She winked at me and hurried to the door. "Good luck with them today. Sorry to dump them on you in their condition and run."

"Well, they'd better be good if they think I'm taking them to Clotilde's for ice cream. Naughty little boys don't get ice cream." I laughed when both boys stopped crying instantly. I mouthed the word "Magic" to Maria.

Maria rushed back and planted a kiss on each of her boys' heads. "Love you all!"

She left and while the boys had stopped crying, they were still cranky and whiny. They fell asleep on the couch while I made them breakfast. The sound of the cartoons on the TV kept me company while my thoughts faded back to Alexei.

I did my best to suppress those thoughts, though. I wouldn't be wise to act on them with him. No matter how forceful he was, I couldn't trust whatever it was Alexei thought he wanted from me. It was always the same with men. They initially swore they could handle the snickers and the stares and the open contempt, but eventually it always ended the same way. A man could only hear the same bullshit so many times before he couldn't help but start to believe it.

After everything that happened in the period of my life I liked to refer to as LBSK (Life Before Sunkissed Key), I had attempted to enter into a few different relationships. I'd learned the hard way that it was impossible for a man to truly trust a woman when he was told over and over again that she was a vicious, backstabbing whore.

Then, there was the added stress of strangers who looked at them with pity. One of my exes had left me because he couldn't handle constantly feeling like a fool.

At the end of the day, for most of the people, I wasn't worth the trouble. My own family had had to distance themselves from me after the show. They were relieved when I'd moved out of state and hundreds of miles away from Rocky Gorge. So, I had no delusions that the same thing wouldn't happen with Alexei. Sure, he would stand up for me in the beginning. They usually did. Being a hero was an ego boost for a while. Defending my honor would get old, though. A man could only fight so many battles before he began to wonder if it was even worth the bother.

No matter how much Alexei thought he wanted me, he didn't know the truth. He didn't know the real me.

If only I could deal with the damned loneliness. Knowing nothing was going to change regarding my relationship status, it almost made me angry that I'd ever met Alexei. I'd been fine before he started making my heart go all aflutter and shit.

I checked on the boys before plating their scrambled eggs and making a conscious effort to shake off my pity party. It wouldn't do me any good. I had two little boys to play with and that was enough. Especially if I took things one day at a time.

I turned the TV off and woke the boys up. "Rise and shine, little monsters! We have a big day ahead of us and it's time to get started."

12

HEIDI

Jonas whined while eating his eggs, but still somehow managed to finish and ask for more. Jaydan just ate in a state of grogginess and most of his eggs ended up on the floor. I let the boys each eat a squeezable yogurt while I gave them baths and got them dressed for the day.

Maria and I had discussed the boys' morning activity schedules and we'd both agreed that it would be beneficial to include educational pursuits. So, our morning was full of learning activities. We colored and played on the beach, but they also listened while I read to them and we worked on the alphabet.

I was proud of how smart and how well rounded they were. They could both sing the entire alphabet song and could write out some of the letters. They were going to be well prepared for entering preschool. In fact, I wasn't trained in early childhood education and they were quickly surpassing what I knew in regards to teaching kids. I'd soon need to do research to keep up with them if they kept sucking up everything I taught them so fast.

I handed them each a half of a sandwich before we left the house, or I knew there was a possibility of hangry tantrums. Then, we were off. I didn't trust them at all in public. I knew them better than that.

While I'd always felt so sorry for children when I saw them in those leash contraptions, after dealing with Jaydan and Jonas in public, I understood the necessity.

Maria didn't use the leash system when she took them out, but they were her kids. If she lost one, they were hers to lose. If I lost one...well, I wasn't taking any chances. Plus, I kind of liked the little brats. I didn't want them getting into any danger.

The leashes weren't as awful as they sounded. They were little monkey shaped backpacks that clicked closed around their little tummies and I looped the ends of the animals' tails onto my wrist. So, technically, the animals were on leashes, not the kids. I still felt slightly awkward about the leashes and I hoped the boys didn't hold it against me when they were older. But, if they did, at least they'd be alive and well while they blamed me in therapy.

We walked down Bluefin Boulevard to Coral Road and then connected to Main Street. Another reason for the leashes, Main Street was sometimes busy enough that I wouldn't trust one of them not to dart out into traffic the moment the opportunity presented.

It was lunchtime and our little island was busy with locals and the tail end of the tourists for the season. We passed plenty of people we knew and made small talk before going on. Outside of Pete's Pets, the boys stopped to pet Pete's big dog, Blossom. We waved at Mann Family Dentistry because, even though Maria couldn't see us, the boys knew where Mommy worked. On the other side of the dentist office was Clotilde's Creamery.

Clotilde had passed years earlier, but her daughter, Cameron, ran the place just as well as her mother had. Clotilde's had a big statue of a cow on top of the building. It was rumored that Clotilde had grown up in Idaho before moving to the Keys and the cow had been modeled after her favorite cow from childhood. I thought all cows looked alike, but apparently the big cow on the roof was the spitting image of Moona Lisa.

Cameron was at the counter when we walked in, the bell over the door announcing our entrance. Despite the customers lined up, Cameron's eyes were drawn to us. "Hey, guys!"

Jayden and Jonas waved to her and pulled me to the counter so they could press their noses up against the glass of the ice cream display and look at all the flavors. They were lost in a world of potential when I felt the air shift around me with another ring of the bell. I looked over my shoulder and couldn't help but smile when Alexei walked in.

He grinned as he sidled up to me, not even bothering to hide his stalking. "I saw you walk in and couldn't stop myself from following."

"Some would consider that creepy."

He stepped closer to me as someone edged by us. "And you?"

I narrowed my eyes at him and fought another stupid smile. "I consider it concerning behavior. You should definitely be checked out."

He held his arms out to the side as though offering himself to me. "Go right ahead."

I laughed and rolled my eyes. I was saved from having to respond by a tug at my hand. I looked down at Jayden and found him watching Alexei. His big blue eyes were curious, the new man presenting an interesting puzzle. I knelt in front of him and held his little waist in my hands while pulling Jonas closer.

"This is Auntie Heidi's friend, Alexei. Have you decided what ice cream you want?"

Jonas nodded and pointed back at the display, not concerned about Alexei. "The pink one."

I grinned. "Good choice! The pink one looks delicious. It's strawberry. You want strawberry?"

Jayden tugged at my hand again and leaned in to whisper in my ear that he wanted the pink one, too. His eyes were still focused on Alexei.

Alexei squatted next to us, his powerful looking thighs stretching his jeans as he did. "Hi. I'm Alexei. I want the pink ice cream, too."

Jonas immediately went to Alexei and held out his arms to be picked up. "You big."

I laughed, surprised at him. There was something deeper than surprise, something warm and fuzzy at seeing Jonas in Alexei's arms, but I ignored it. "We don't tell people they're big, Jonas."

Jayden had watched silently, but suddenly, he wanted Alexei to hold him, too. I pursed my lips, not enjoying being an outcast in my own group. Alexei, wearing an ear to ear grin, easily picked up Jayden, too, holding each boy in a thickly muscled arm. His expression was one of victory.

I watched them for a second while he leaned them over the case, showing them the ice cream closer up. Part of me worried that Maria would be pissed about a stranger holding her boys, but for some stupid reason, I trusted Alexei. They weren't my kids, though.

As if she'd been reading my mind, Maria popped into the shop. She waved at Cameron and then came over to us. Her eyes raked over Alexei and then focused on me. I could tell she had something brewing behind those brown eyes and when she got closer, I could see it was mischief. "Hi, babies!"

Jayden and Jonas waved at their mother, still content to remain up high in Alexei's arms. I nervously tucked my hair behind my ears, feeling flustered at being caught out with her kids and a man that she didn't know. "Hey! We came to get ice cream and ran into a friend."

She wagged her eyebrows at me. "Uh huh."

Alexei extended a hand, despite having the kids wiggling in his arms. "I'm Alexei. You're their mother?"

Maria grinned. "I am. Maria. You must be the reason my best friend has been so mysterious lately? She's all daydreams and secret little smiles, but she won't breathe a word about why."

He met my eyes and a heated expression passed over his face. "I hope so. I've been trying my hardest."

I groaned while Maria floated away on some romantic cloud. *Lord have mercy.*

13

ALEXEI

Heidi was in a short sun dress that showed her long, smooth legs. The dress was yellow with little white flowers all over it. The swells of her breasts were showing just slightly over the scooping neckline of the dress. Her toes were painted a seashell pink and her fingernails matched. Her thick, wavy caramel colored hair was tied in a ponytail and everything about her made me think thoughts and feel feelings I had no business thinking and feeling while holding two innocent little boys in my arms.

Spotting her had been a happy accident. I'd been grabbing lunch for the team, but after seeing Heidi slip into the ice cream shop, I'd quickly decided it wouldn't hurt them to go without a meal. Watching her interact with the two little boys had been an extra perk. She was sexy as hell, and so beautiful that she stole my breath. Observing her motherly interactions with the children stole my heart.

Fuck, I sounded like a teen romance, but there it was. Heart stolen. It was the moment that I *knew*—without a doubt I knew. She was my mate. My bear had been in love with her since day one, minute one. I supposed it took me longer because I couldn't believe that it'd been so easy to find her. There was no arguing it, though.

Standing in that ice cream shop, I knew it just as well as I knew my name. She was the one.

Maria cleared her throat and I realized I was standing there staring at Heidi amidst an awkward silence. Maria broke the silence. "I've got to get back to work. I just ran over because I saw you walk past the dental office with my little guys."

Heidi pulled her friend a few steps away, her eyes still on me. She whispered something privately, but I was a shifter. I had amazing hearing. "I'm sorry, Maria. I didn't plan this. If you're uncomfortable with the boys being around someone you don't know, I'll tell him to go."

Maria scoffed. "You act like I don't trust you. Those are practically your kids, too, Heidi. Judging by the way you look at him, you like him. So, I do too."

Heidi's cheeks tinged pink, but she just rolled her eyes and waved her friend off. "Want me to get something for you while I'm out?"

"Would you? I had a couple of people schedule for this afternoon, so I won't be home for a little while."

The little boys wiggled in my arms and one of them tugged at my hair. "Ice cream?"

I grinned at him. "I get it. It's hard to wait while the grownups stand around talking, isn't it?"

Heidi came back to my side and glanced back at Maria. She mouthed something and then looked up at me, face red still. "Sorry about that. I just had to ask her something."

I looked down at her, impressed with the way she put the kids first. Cocky, or not, I thought she wanted to see me. Yet, she was willing to send me away if Maria was uncomfortable with a random man hanging out with her kids.

"Ice cream!"

She cocked her head to the side and gave the screaming boy a look that said she disapproved. "We don't scream for things we want."

He pouted at her and big tears welled up in his eyes. "Ice cream."

"Remember the magic word? Can you say please?" When the

little ones both said please, she smiled, her face lighting up. "That's better. Now, we're still all getting pink?"

"So *that's* the magic word! I've been wracking my brain for the right word to get you to go out with me." I winked at her and laughed when she gave me an exasperated look.

It felt strange to be standing there, two kids in my arms, waiting on my mate to order our ice cream. And by strange, I meant wonderful. It wasn't hard to look at her and imagine a future with more of this in it. I liked Sunkissed Key. It was hot, yeah, but I could deal. Heidi and I could buy our own house here and start a family of our own. I liked the idea of it. Matter of fact, I loved the idea.

"I'll pay. Just grab my wallet." I turned so she could see my wallet in my back pocket.

"Nice try. I'll pay." She did just that, chatting with the woman at the register one minute, holding four cones stacked high with ice cream, the next. "Come on, guys. We can eat outside."

The boys were suddenly wild animals in my arms. Shrieking and wiggling to get free and run. The slippery little guys were like greased piglets. I held on, ending up with my arms around their waists, holding them parallel to the ground. They let loose laugh-like squeals that I wasn't sure was good until Heidi turned and laughed with them.

I held onto them for dear life until we got outside and I managed to put the boys on their feet. Heidi still had them by their...leashes? I made a face. "Are they on leashes?"

She handed them their cones and nodded. "I'm not losing them. They're like little magicians who can vanish with the snap of their little fingers. I'm not chancing anything in public."

I held our cones as she settled them into a chair together, right up next to her. She even tied the ends of their leashes to her arm before reaching for her ice cream.

"So, this is your day job?"

She nodded. "Yeah. I babysit and help Maria around her house during the day. Then, I bartend at night."

"You're busy." I licked the tip of my ice cream and nearly groaned when her heated eyes followed the motion.

Instead of replying, she just nodded and looked away. Then, she licked her cone, completely unaware of the torture she was putting me through. Her tongue stroked the cone in ways that my mind would not ever forget. I adjusted myself in my chair and forced my eyes away.

"Oh, crap."

I looked over and saw that she'd gotten ice cream all down her hand somehow. She passed me the leashes and stood up. "I'm getting napkins. Are you okay with them for a second?"

I nodded and looked at the boys. "We're good, right guys?"

They ignored me, the ice cream was far more captivating. I held their leashes and watched Heidi walk inside, a big smile on her face. She'd just grabbed a stack of napkins and turned to head back out when a woman stepped up to her and said something that made the joyful expression on Heidi's face drop like a lead balloon. The woman's expression was a snarl of disgust and anger and she poked her index finger into Heidi's chest as she spoke.

It was over in seconds, and Heidi returned with the napkins, her eyes misty. Her smile was gone and she looked flustered with her face red and her mouth pinched tightly.

"You okay?" I didn't realize I was standing until the boys cried out. I was pulling their kid-leashes too tightly.

She nodded and took the leashes from me. "We're going to go home. Come on, Jayden, Jonas. You can eat your ice cream on the walk home."

"Hold on, Heidi. Talk to me. What happened?" My stomach was in my throat and I wasn't sure what to do to help.

"It's nothing. See you later." And then she was leaving, rushing the kids off with trembling hands.

14

ALEXEI

Unable to let her leave like that, I went after her. I caught her arm and pulled her to a stop. When I saw that she was crying, I felt my bear rage inside me. "Come on. My office is right down here."

She let me scoop the boys up and pull her with me. Her hand gripped mine tightly and I could hear her heart racing. We were passing the ice cream shop again when the same woman who'd upset her initially stepped out and scowled. Heidi froze.

"Is that someone else's husband you've got your hooks into? Shame on you!" The woman's voice was harsh and cruel, her eyes just as condescending.

I put myself between the two woman and looked down at Heidi. "Come on, Heidi."

She shook her head. "We've really got to get home. I have something to do that I just remembered."

I felt my blood boil as she took the boys from me, a distressed look on her face. Before I had a chance to argue, she was rushing away, a child in each arm, sticky little hands in her hair, and ice cream dripping down one of the boy's cones and onto her shoulder.

Spinning around to face the woman who'd hurt my mate, I found her staring after Heidi with a vicious scowl on her face. I didn't like to yell at woman. I didn't like to hurt women. Of course, in my line of work, there were exceptions. I'd dealt with women who could make Osama Bin Laden look like Mickey Mouse. With the sour woman before me, I was sorely tempted to snatch her up by her ankles and shake her.

"Who are you?" My voice was barely more than a growl and when the offending woman heard it, she stepped back.

"It doesn't matter who I am." She shook her head but took another step back concerned for her safety. "Are you married?"

I frowned, confused by the woman's obsession with marriage. "Of course not! What's your deal, lady? What do you just go around spewing vitriol and hurting people?"

"Me? ME? Don't you know who she is? She's the one who hurts people. A shameless hussy who breaks up marriages with her selfishness."

It was my turn to step back. The venom coming out of the woman was overwhelming. "What are you talking about?"

"That's Heidi Garcia from *Love In An Instant*. The TV show?" She rolled her eyes. "She was on the first season that came out. She's a monster. She slept with people's boyfriends, just to cause trouble. Her motto was something about being a slut and proud of it and she certainly showed the world her true colors. A complete trollop."

I saw red and stepped closer to her. I lowered my voice and growled at her. "Watch your mouth. You're behaving this way because of something you saw in a TV show? You're the one who should be ashamed of yourself. I would say that you're lucky you're a lady, but I think we both know that you're no lady. So, I'll say you're lucky I'm a gentleman."

She blanched, her anger instantly replaced by fear. When I growled again for good measure, she whimpered and scurried away.

I shook my head and ran my hands through my hair. I wasn't proud to have threatened her, but what the fuck? She'd just verbally attacked my mate for something on a TV show?

I made my way back to the near-empty office and was glad to see Hannah inside. I dropped into the chair in front of her and sighed.

"Whoa. What's up, Alexei? I don't think I've ever seen you frown before."

Megan's head popped out from the back office. She looked at me and her eyes widened. Kerrigan's head popped out right below Megan's. She slapped her hand over her chest and hurried out. "Oh, my gosh! What's wrong, Alexei?"

Their mates, Serge, Roman, and Dmitry, stepped into the main office, their faces masks of confusion, too. Serge shook his head, like he was trying to clear it. "What happened to you?"

"You guys ever heard of a show called *Love In An Instant*?"

Hannah nodded. "Yeah, why?"

"I met someone from it, I guess." I hesitated. "What is it?"

Dmitry mock saluted. "I'm out of here. I'm going back to work."

Roman settled next to his mate. "I've got nothing better to do."

"This isn't important, then?" Serge held up his hands when I growled at him. "I meant *work* important. It's not *work*-related, then?"

Hannah shushed her mate and turned back to me. "It's a reality dating show. The biggest one on TV. They put together groups of people to see what happens and film it, basically. I mean, they pair you up with someone based on some kind of test you take, but then it's kind of this free for all. They try to pretend like it's this love at first sight thing, but it's just a ploy to watch people fool around and make asses of themselves. I mean, no one ever sticks with the person they're matched with.

"Who'd you meet from it?"

I frowned, not understanding most of what she said. My brain was trying to relate it to Heidi and what I knew about her but it wasn't computing. "Heidi Garcia."

Hannah's mouth fell open. "Holy shit."

"What?"

"Even I know this part." Megan shook her head and moved nearer to Roman who pulled her into his lap. She let out a startled, "Oof," but didn't lose focus on the conversation. "That poor girl."

I sat up straight and felt my bear fighting to get loose. He wanted to fight for his mate. "Tell me."

"The show has this cult-like following. There are so many people who think it's real and they are obsessed with it. Well, Heidi was the villain on her season. I don't know how much was real and how much was staged for dramatic effect, but to say she was not nice to the other women on the show would be a huge understatement."

Hannah nodded. "I mean, like Megan said, who knows if it was real, but if it wasn't, that's even more messed up. She was painted as a complete evil bitch."

"Well, yeah." Megan made a face. "When that one couple that everyone loved, Aaron and Ashley, were about to get engaged and they were the sweethearts of prime time TV, she was caught in bed with Aaron."

"I read something on Yahoo News a while back. A 'where are they now' type of thing. No info on Heidi. Apparently, or so the article stated, she was so hated after the show that she couldn't get any other work. She actually received death threats and just kind of vanished."

I stood up and slammed my hand down on the desk in front of me. "It's all bullshit. She's sweet and kind. When we were getting ice cream, she was confronted by some woman whose face looked like she'd just been sucking lemons. Heidi turned away, nearly in tears."

Roman growled at me, but it was just a warning to not yell at his mate. Megan patted Roman on the chest to placate him and gave me a warm smile. "Sorry, Alexei. Is she..."

"She's my mate." I stood straighter when I said it, filled with pride. No matter what they said, I knew what kind of person Heidi was. "And she's not an evil bitch. Not by a long shot."

Hannah smiled. "Well, she is gorgeous, I'll say that. She reminds me of, whose that actress from the show *Empire*?"

Megan nodded. "Nicole Ari Parker! She has the same coloring and they're both rare beauties."

"Yes! Nicole Ari Parker. I feel bad for Heidi. Even if she had been that person in the past, it doesn't give anyone the right to attack her. Everyone has a past."

I raked my hands through my hair and crossed my arms over my chest. "I don't like seeing her upset."

Roman grunted. "Welcome to the club, brother. Get ready to suffer for a while. Until it sorts itself out, anyway."

15

HEIDI

Work was hard that night. I wanted to call off and hide out at home, but there was no one who could cover my shift and I wasn't going to leave Mimi with the whole bar by herself. I was in a terrible mood though. I knew that I wasn't making anyone's night with my saltiness. I just couldn't shake my mood. Hearing that woman insult me so thoroughly at Clotilde's had thrown me. It hit me harder than normal because I was there with Alexei and the boys. They could've overheard the vile things she'd said about me.

It wasn't fair. I wanted to scream back at everyone who taunted me and reminded me of that stupid show. I'd done that in the beginning—flipped out and told them how I felt, but I'd since learned. It never changed anything. No one cared about the truth. They had their opinion and that was that. I could scream until I was blue in the face about how it was a fake TV show, how we were all following prompts and director's cues and everything was staged to make for good television, but they'd never believe me. My name was tainted. I was labeled a whore and a homewrecker. The Cuban slut, people called me. And, hell, they knew all about it, or so they thought, since they'd seen it with their own eyes.

If I knew when I'd signed on what that show would end up doing to my life, I would've run as fast as humanly possible to get away. I'd just seen it as a way to jump start my fledgling acting career. I thought that if I did the show, I could get an agent and, subsequently, some better gigs. Little did I know, I'd never get a call back again. I was branded by the character I played—a nasty, bitchy troublemaker. I would have accepted being typecast as a villain, but it was worse. Producers and casting directors assumed that I really was a difficult person, like the character, and that I'd be hell to work with. No one would come within a hundred yards of me.

At the end of the day, the missed career opportunity was fine. I was happy being a small-town girl in the Florida Keys—a bartender and babysitter. It was the harassment and judgement from fans of the show that I couldn't handle. And it would usually pop up from out of left field, like the woman in the ice cream shop.

I'd never actually slept with anyone from that show. I hadn't done any of the things I was continually accused of. I was just a foolish kid who'd mistakenly thought people wouldn't actually believe that reality TV was, well, reality.

My stomach ached from knowing that Alexei was going to hear those things sooner or later, and that he'd already heard some of them. I knew that I had no business worrying about what he thought of me. I had no intention of developing any type of relationship with him beyond a very casual friendship. I couldn't. That was how it had to be and that was *fine*. Everything was fine.

"Are you with me, Heidi?"

I snapped out of my trance, and turned to Sarah. "Sorry, what'd you need?"

She called out her order again and frowned. "You okay, girl?"

I nodded and started working on the drinks. I wasn't up to my usual self, but I was still faster than most bartenders. When I handed the drinks over to her, she was still frowning. "I'm good."

She looked away and then grinned. "Hottie's back for you."

I knew it was Alexei before I even looked. Sure enough, he was leaning against the end of the bar, looking every bit as handsome as I was trying to forget he was. He made it impossible.

The bar wasn't packed, but it was busy enough that I had to stop and pour drinks twice before I reached him. I was nervous. I'd left abruptly earlier and I was embarrassed. Who knew what he thought of me?

I had to remind myself that I wasn't supposed to care.

"Hey." He leaned towards me, his face drawn into a tight smile. It looked like he'd combed his hair. It was neatly brushed back from his face, a contrast to the shadow of stubble on his face that hadn't been touched. He was in a button-down shirt, jeans, and work boots. He looked like he'd just come off a modeling shoot and I loved it.

I swallowed an excessive amount of drool and reminded myself once again that nothing was allowed to happen between the two of us. "Hi."

He leaned even farther across the bar and his hand came up to gently brush a strand of hair out of my face. "Did I mention earlier that that dress is killer on you?"

I wanted to turn my face into his hand, but I resisted and he pulled it back into his own space. "You don't give up."

"Never." He rested his elbows on the bar and his smile was just as tight as ever. "You okay?"

I shrugged. "I'm fine."

"You don't look fine. You look like you could use a drink yourself."

I saw a hand go out with an empty glass down at the other end of the bar and nodded at it. "Sorry, I have to work."

It went like that for about an hour. He nursed the one beer he'd ordered and tried to talk to me between customers. He seemed genuinely worried about me and it was hard to face.

"What's a guy gotta do to get some attention around here?" Alexei grinned at me over his beer, the look on his face more determined than happy. "I mean, I dressed up for you."

I took his warm beer from him and gave him a cold one. "Is that all for me?"

He unbuttoned another button on his shirt then gave me a sexy, exaggerated pout like he was on the cover of GQ or something and winked. "This better?"

I rolled my eyes. "You can't possibly like this."

"Being ignored by the prettiest woman in the bar while I make a fool of myself to make her smile? What's not to like about that?"

"I'm fine, Alexei. Go home."

"Not without getting a genuine smile from you."

"Look, I've had a shit day. It's not a big deal. People have them."

"I know people have them, but I don't like that *you're* having one. I don't care about anyone else."

I stopped mid-pour of a tequila shot. Looking up at him, I couldn't help tilting my head to the side and trying to see him clearer. Had he just implied that he cared about me? Naw. He didn't know me.

"I'm not giving up. I'll dance on this damn bar if I have to."

"You can't dance on the bar."

"I can."

"It's against the rules."

"Do I look like I follow rules?"

I sighed. "Alexei, you don't have to worry about me."

He stood up and grabbed the edge of the bar. "You're really gonna make me do this?"

"You're not getting up there."

"Watch me."

16

ALEXEI

Heidi slapped her hands over her eyes when I swung up onto the bar and stood to my full height. I knocked my head on the ceiling, and a few colorful toothpicks fell off, but that didn't stop me. I wasn't going to stop until she smiled and I saw the pain in her eyes fade. If I knew one thing, it was that she didn't deserve her suffering and I'd do everything in my power to take it from her. That was two things, but I knew them both.

"Turn up the music!" I'd never danced on a bar before. But, hey, I'd try almost anything once.

Someone obliged and as the music got louder there was chanting and clapping as well as a few hoots and hollers. I ignored the hands waving dollar bills in the air. With plenty of eyes on me and nothing to do but entertain, I did just that. I moved to the music as best as I could, but I was a fucking bear shifter. Dancing wasn't in my DNA.

"Don't avert your eyes, Heidi. This is all for you!" I swung my hips and accidentally kicked someone's beer off the bar. "Sorry, man."

Heidi looked up at me, her hands cupped on either side of her face, like she wasn't sure what to do. "Get down! You're going to get kicked out!"

I unbuttoned a few more buttons. "What did you say? You want to see more skin?! Why, Heidi! I'm shocked!"

She shook her head and turned her back to me. "I'm not watching this!"

I unbuttoned the rest of the shirt and laughed when she looked over her shoulder and through her fingers at me before turning away again. "I'm not stopping until you smile."

She swung around and flashed her teeth at me. "There. Now, get down."

"Oh, but that wasn't a genuine smile. Nice try, though. I guess I'll just have to lose the pants."

She turned to face me, a real smile twisting her lips. "You're such an idiot."

I grinned back at her. "And you're the most amazing woman I've ever met."

"Come down from there."

I hopped off, onto her side of the bar, and smiled down at her. I was probably standing too close, pushing too hard. "You're beautiful."

"You're crazy." She hesitated, looked around, and then met my eyes. "Sometimes, you have to let people feel how they feel. Even if it isn't what you want."

I bit my lip and took a step back. "You're right. I apologize."

She shocked me by stepping into my space. "This wasn't one of those times."

"Heidi…"

She took my hand and stepped around me, pulling me after her. Through a swinging door, away from the bar, down a hallway, and into a small room with a desk and a chair that was missing a wheel. She pushed me until my back hit the wall behind me and then she moved closer, until she was a breath away.

I grabbed her waist and pulled her the rest of the way into my body. She fit just right against me, her curves soft and tempting. I stared down into her eyes, looking for any sign that she was opposed to what we were doing. There was nothing but fevered heat staring back at me, though.

I don't know who kissed who first. We both moved and then our mouths were sliding together and her taste was exploding on my mouth like a professional firework show. Her mouth was soft and hungry against mine. Her hands were on my face, holding me while our tongues entwined.

I wrapped my arms around her, pulling her tighter against me, and kissed her deeper. She even tasted sugary sweet. I moaned when she took my bottom lip between her teeth and nipped.

The kiss was intense and powerful. The only thing I was sure of in that moment was wanting more of her. Her fingers ran through my hair, grasping it, pulling me closer. I slipped my hands down over her ass and easily lifted her up against my body. Her thighs locked around my waist so our bodies pressed up flush against one another from shoulders to hips.

Her ass was firm in my hands, the rounded cheeks filling my palms perfectly. When I flexed my fingers, squeezing, her kiss grew wilder, and she moaned into my mouth.

I ran a hand up her back and gripped the back of her neck, holding her steady and moving us over until she was laid out on the desk and I was standing between her thighs. She opened her legs wider and I gripped them harder than I had to, but I had never been so turned on. Her skin was soft and silky, and it drove me insane. All of her drove me insane. I wanted to touch and taste every inch of her a million times over.

Heidi dragged my mouth back to hers, and I closed the gap that her thighs had made for me, feeling her heat through my jeans as I rocked my erection against her.

Her nails dug into my shoulders and she locked her ankles behind my lower back. Her mouth open, breathing heavily, she met my eyes with a half-lidded, needy gaze.

Holding eye contact, watching every nuance of her expression, I rocked my hips into her again and again until I knew the rhythm she wanted. Then, I gripped the back of her neck once more and held onto her hip with my free hand and rolled my hips against her while pressing my forehead to hers and breathing through gritted teeth.

Heidi in the throes of passion was the most erotic thing I'd ever seen. She wanted me. Her body was desperate for me. And the sentiment was mutual—I wanted her just as badly.

Heidi held onto me tighter as her small moans became higher pitched and breathier. Suddenly, she clenched her thighs tighter around me and her nails dug into my back. Her neck tensed under my hand and her body arched into me like a longbow. Her head dropped to my shoulder and her teeth clamped down on my shoulder as a muffled cry sounded.

As I felt her orgasm rock through her, I gripped her tighter, feeling my own release too close. I wasn't about to come in my pants and embarrass myself like a teenager. I squeezed my eyes shut and inhaled deeply. The scent of my mate's arousal was one I never wanted to forget.

"Hey, Hei—" A woman's voice abruptly cut off and a giggle followed. "Sorry! Never mind! Didn't see a thing!"

Heidi pulled back and covered her face with her hands. "Shit."

I pulled her hands away and kissed her, feeling her shiver against me. "I'm not done with you."

17

HEIDI

I slept better that night than I had since meeting Alexei. I felt like all the tension in my body had drained away and I was finally feeling at ease. At least, my body was. My brain was in a bit of a tailspin, but it wasn't enough to keep me up.

I got to the beach bright and early that next morning, fishing pole in one hand, tackle box in the other. I hadn't had my usual fresh fish dinner in a few days and I wanted some kind of normalcy back in my life. I'd already caught my dinner by the time Houdini showed up.

I should have been pissed at Mr. Zoo for being so goddamned lax that an almost 900 pound bear was able to repeatedly slip out of his supposedly secure sanctuary. But I was too excited to see my bear to be angry. I hurried down to the beach and he knocked me back on my ass in the sand and then covered my face in sloppy kisses. I laughed and gently pushed his huge face away. It went on like that for a few minutes. He was so excited to see me that he rubbed against me until he settled down beside me. Then, I wrapped my arm around him, as much as I could, and I leaned into him.

I talked to him more than I talked to anyone else. It was super weird, but there wasn't much about the entire situation that wasn't crazy, so why not just go for it? He listened. That was the kicker. The damn polar bear listened better than a best friend. He watched me as I spoke and seemed to reply with his little sounds when appropriate. I should've been more worried that I'd lost mind, probably.

That morning, I told him all about Alexei. I told him about the mean woman and then Alexei doing everything he could to cheer me up, including dancing on the bar and pretending he was going to strip. I couldn't remember anyone ever trying so hard for me—or caring like that. Finally, I told him about kissing Alexei. The kissing that had turned quickly to dry humping and then an earth-shaker of an orgasm. I left the orgasm part out, slightly red faced as I thought about it.

"And then Sarah walked in on us. Of course, she was like a dog with a bone during closing. She wanted to know everything." I sighed. "There's nothing to know, though. I don't know anything about Alexei. I mean, I know that he's funny and hot, and I know that he seems like a nice guy. I don't know anything else, though."

I grinned when Houdini put his big paw on my back and patted me. The things he'd learned in whatever circus he'd been rescued from were amazing. It was almost like sitting next to a person the way he responded and interacted.

"Thanks." I reached up to scratch his ear. "I'm just freaked out, I guess. I've been alone for so long that I've gotten used to it being that way. It's not easy to learn to trust someone. I don't know his motives. I don't know anything. And who's to say he won't be like every other man. It's not easy to have random people pop up and proclaim that the woman you're dating is a slut. It doesn't matter that I'm not. It can get to a person over time. Especially a man.

"I don't know if I have it in me to open myself up to more pain. And Alexei would be a hard man to not miss if he ran."

I hugged my knees and watched as a seagull landed close by, spotted Houdini, and then freaked out before flying off. Houdini huffed next to me and got to his feet. He paced back and forth in front of me, his head raising to let out little growls every so often. If I didn't know better, I'd have said it looked like he was trying to lecture me.

"It looks like we're both stuck in our feelings this morning."

He looked at me and actually rolled his eyes. Then, like he was tired of me, he strolled away, towards the sanctuary.

"Hey!" I got up and hurried after him. "What are you doing?"

He just trotted along until he got to the wildlife sanctuary's back gate and then he used his head to crudely knock on it himself. I just stood there, mouth open, and watched as he disappeared inside the gate and it shut in my face.

I stood there for a few seconds, unsure of what had just happened. Well, it did make sense in a way that he'd know his way back. And maybe he was hungry or something. Or maybe he was sick of hearing me complain about my complicated love life.

I strolled slowly back to the beach to get my fishing gear. I was still lost in my thoughts when the sound of footsteps approaching dragged me back to the present. I looked up and spotted Alexei jogging towards me. My mouth dropped open.

He was in nothing but a pair of low slung swim trunks, and holy mother of god, his hair was wet and wild; his body dripped water as he advanced. Muscles flexed and worked as he ran, all of them jaw-dropping.

"Close your mouth or you'll catch flies." He grinned and stopped in my space. He cupped my face and leaned down. His eyes flicked to my mouth and then back up. "Hi."

I swallowed, my brain needed the second of time to try to catch up. "You're wet."

He laughed. "Yeah, I am."

"You don't have many clothes on."

"Want to even the playing field?"

I rolled my eyes and stepped back, his joke giving me the chance to snap back to myself. "You're a smartass."

"And you're a goddess. Let me take you to breakfast?"

"I have work. Besides you're nearly naked. I know the dress code is pretty lax around the island, but what you're wearing—or not wearing—might be pushing it."

"Lunch then. I'll wear more clothes, promise." He wagged his brows. "Though, are you sure you want me to?"

Laughing, I looked up at him, trying to see through the exterior to what he really wanted underneath. I was nervous. It was easy to forget reality when he was in front of me, but it was still there. I felt as though I liked him, despite not knowing him. It scared me to think about how I would feel if I got to know him and it turned out disastrously. What if I liked him too much and he wanted nothing else to do with me?

Like he could read my mind, he caught my hands in his and smiled gently. "Just lunch. We can talk, get to know each other. We'll take a step back from last night. I'm good with that."

I licked my lips, still nervous, but nodded. I couldn't help it. I did want to know more. "Okay. I can meet you at one o'clock."

"Bayfront Diner okay with you?"

I nodded. Looking up at him, I felt something so familiar in his eyes, the way he watched so patiently. Nodding my head, I backed away. "See you at one."

He smiled and watched me go. "I could walk you home."

"Don't press your luck."

He laughed. "See you at one."

18

ALEXEI

Part of me felt guilty for using the things Heidi told me to get her to open up to me, but I had the best intentions. She was my mate and I wanted to be with her. I wanted her to learn that she could trust me. The end would justify the means.

She sat across from me at the diner, eyes cautious but curious as they flitted between me and the menu. She'd changed into another dress, a white one. The neckline was higher, but her shoulders were mostly bare and I found I was attracted by any skin she showed.

It must have been Kerrigan's day off since Susie popped up next to us, her expression revealing her own curiosity. "Well, well. It's been a minute since you've come by, Alexei."

The older woman patted my hand and smiled. "I've been busy with work, or you know I'd stop in more often."

She turned her eyes on Heidi. "And you, missy. You don't come by nearly enough. I can see your house from the front window. Yet, you never stop in and say hello."

"Oh, Susie, I'm sorry. I don't eat out much anymore." She grinned at the older woman. "Besides, you know I had an issue with your cooking. I couldn't stop eating it. Pretty sure I gained ten pounds from your cinnamon rolls alone."

Susie wagged her finger. "Well, it looks like you could use some. Put a little more meat on those bones."

Heidi laughed, a full laugh that drew the attention of people around us. It was infectious. "That's funny. You're a real hoot."

"Uh huh. Anyway. Sweet tea for both of you?" When we nodded, she walked off, just to come right back with a basket of cinnamon rolls. "Eat up."

I grinned at Heidi and then laughed when she stared hungrily at the rolls. "I didn't mean for you to have some kind of pastry crisis over lunch."

She sighed heavily and met my eyes. "I love these things more than almost anything in the world. It's a downward spiral, though."

"I'm sure you were still stunning with ten pounds of pastry weight."

"You have to say that. You're trying to get into my pants." She hesitated. "At least I think that's what you're trying to do."

"Amongst other things."

"What are the other things? Cue me in on the plan."

I leaned into her and plucked out a roll. "You'd think I was crazy."

"Try me."

"I'm not looking for a hook up. Not anymore." I took a bite of the roll and licked my lips. "I want more. In fact I'd like to see you with ten extra pounds of weight provided I was the one with you on all the dates where you ate enough to gain that much."

Her eyes went wide and she sank back in the booth. "You're not being serious."

I nodded. "I am."

"You don't even know me."

"I know enough." I shrugged. "Well, I don't know enough. I want to know more. There's a reason I keep showing up. I want to know you. I want you to know me."

"I don't date."

"Because of the cinnamon roll thing?"

She laughed suddenly, her face lighting up and the worry lines around her eyes fading. "No, not because of that. Because of...other stuff."

"A husband? Kids? You're actually a serial killer and afraid a relationship might blow your cover?"

"You're a smartass." She was still smiling, though. "Mostly because of stuff like that what happened with that woman at Clotilde's Creamery."

"You don't date because random psychos might come up and harass you? To be fair, I think having me next to you with a big snarl on my face would go a long way towards preventing those types of encounters. I do a mean growl, too."

"Alexei—"

I snarled and let out a loud growl. When half the diners turned to stare, I crossed my eyes and made a crazy face at them. "See? No one would fuck with you with me next to you, looking like this."

She laughed again and hid behind her menu. "You're nuts, you know? You're the strangest person."

"I'm not the one with a pastry problem." I leaned over the table and caught her hand. "I'm serious, though. I'm not into hooking up and running away. I'm not going anywhere, Heidi, not unless you really want me to."

She looked away for a second, a serious look settling over her face. When she met my gaze again, her expression was determined. "I don't date."

"Fine. You win. We won't date. We'll hang out until you decide you want more." I felt my body heat as she licked her lips. "We'll have to discuss whether we're doing a just friends or a friends with benefits thing though."

Her cheeks burned. "You're stubborn."

"I like you. There's something here and I'm not going to just turn away as though you aren't worth fighting for."

Susie came back over and took our orders, silently pushing the rolls closer to Heidi the whole time. By the time she left, the rolls were practically in Heidi's lap.

"Why?"

I raised my eyebrows at Heidi. "Why what?"

"Why are you so interested in me?"

"Some things are bigger than us. Fate, for one."

"And you think this is..." she gestured back and forth between us, "*fate*?"

I shrugged. "Something like that."

19

HEIDI

I was floating on a weird high that night at the bar. I couldn't stop thinking about everything Alexei had said. He thought we were supposed to be together—like through the guiding hand of fate or something. That sentiment was strangely romantic for a man. I liked it. It still scared me a little to fall for him only to have my past turn out to be too much for him in the end. But, I kind of knew what he was saying. I had this strange feeling like we were connected, too. I felt something so familiar when I looked at him.

It made it hard not to want to throw out every conviction I had about remaining single. Alexei made me feel hopeful, like maybe things could be different. Hell, one afternoon spent with him and I was having trouble not imagining waking up next to him every day.

I was excited, but scared. I couldn't help feeling giddy and eager for what was going to happen next, but I had made myself into a pessimist over the past decade. That didn't vanish with a little attention from a hot guy. Something had to be wrong with the picture. Right?

I didn't know. I was confused.

The bar was busy and I'd been working for a few hours already.

Alexei had already told me he had to work and wouldn't be able to stop in that night. Yet, I found myself still looking for him.

Stupid? Yep. Could I help it? Nope.

Lord, I had it bad.

When the three women settled at the bar, I felt a shiver of unease as their eyes raked over me. It wasn't so much judgement as it was curiosity on their part. I knew that they recognized me, though. More than from just around town. And, if I wasn't mistaken, I recognized one. She had owned a photography shop at the end of the island. The place had been leveled by the hurricane.

I put a smile on my face, despite feeling like I was walking into a trap. "Hey, what can I get you ladies?"

The one I recognized smiled brightly at me and stuck out her hand. "Hi. I'm Megan."

Another chimed in. "I'm Hannah. And this is Kerrigan. We're friends of Alexei."

After I'd shaken their hands, I just kind of stepped back and looked at them. I didn't know what to expect. Did they just want to meet me or were they there to warn me away from their so-called friend? Also, why did Alexei have so many female friends?

"We're all mates to other guys in P.O.L.A.R.—his task force." Hannah shrugged. "I doubt you've met any of the guys yet, though."

I shook my head. "Um, nope."

"You have no clue what we're talking about, do you?" Megan laughed lightly. "Alexei hasn't mentioned us? Or, maybe you two haven't had much time to talk." She waggled her eyebrows.

I bristled. *Here come the slut slurs.*

"I just mean that it's a mate thing. It's not uncommon to meet, screw like rabbits, and save the conversations for later." Megan nodded to the other women. "We've all been there."

I stared at her. What the hell was she talking about?

Kerrigan nodded. "She's not wrong."

"The joys of being mated to polar bear shifters." Hannah smiled a secret little smile.

My head snapped back like she'd slapped me. What the fuck were they talking about? Polar... I thought of Houdini. Was that a coincidence?

"What's wrong?" Megan's face wrinkled in concern. "Are you okay?"

"What are you all talking about?" I gripped the bar top and shook my head. "Why did you say 'polar bear'?"

Their faces all blanched at once. Kerrigan's eyes seemed to grow even larger behind her thick glasses. Megan's jaw dropped and Hannah gasped. It was Megan who spoke, though. "We... You don't know any of this, do you?"

"Any of what? What about polar bears?"

"Shit." Megan looked at the women on either side of her and muttered another curse. "I'm so sorry. We just assumed... Alexei has been spending so much time with you and he's even happier than normal. We just thought the two of you had already mated..."

I had a second to try to digest what she'd said before Hannah piped up. "We shouldn't have come. We shouldn't have said anything."

"He's going to kill us." Kerrigan groaned. "And he'll have every right to. I'm sorry, too. It wasn't our place to tell you."

"Tell me what?" I was getting pissed, feeling like I was the outsider in an insider's club.

"Alexei will tell you everything."

I stepped closer to them. "The three of you need to spill. You've already started, no way I'm letting you walk out of here without an explanation. I especially want to know why you mentioned polar bears."

Megan groaned. "Promise you won't be mad at him? He would've told you himself if we hadn't opened our big mouths."

I couldn't promise that. I was already upset and I hadn't even heard them out yet. I had a feeling I was going to be royally pissed at Alexei once I had.

I waved Mimi over and told her I needed to take my break immediately. She covered the bar while I went to a table in the back with the three women. All of them looked stressed and were casing the exits as though they might just decide to make a run for it instead. They didn't, though. I motioned for them to be seated, and when they were, I took a chair facing the three of them.

I eyed them sternly. "Spill."

"We didn't come to ruin anything between you two. We're not like that, honest. We just wanted to meet you. Alexei has been over the moon and he mentioned it was you he'd been spending time with, so we wanted to..."

"You wanted to see if I was really the bitchy, homewrecking whore from TV? I know you know who I am. I saw it all over your faces when you walked in."

Megan raised her hands in protest. "No! Alexei is a great guy and he wouldn't have a mate like that. Really." She looked at the other two as if wanting one of them to interject, but neither said anything. "We just wanted to welcome you to the fold, so to speak."

"The fold?" I frowned. "Fine. Explain all of this to me, though. The polar bear talk. There's been a polar bear running loose on South Beach. I've returned him the Sunkissed Wildlife Sanctuary several times now and he keeps getting loose again. I'm suddenly pretty damned sure that it's no coincidence that you three happened to bring up a polar bear. Is this about him?"

Hannah winced. "Um...okay, unless there is something really crazy happening on this island, that polar bear is Alexei."

I leaned back in my chair and sighed. "Is this some kind of prank? You all think it's funny to come in and mess with me?"

"No! No. It's nothing like that. Our mates, our men, are shapeshifters. I know it sounds crazy, but they have the ability to transform into polar bears. All of them. So, the polar bear you've encountered on South Beach? Probably Alexei."

"That's ridiculous."

"I thought so, too. Until I saw my mate, Roman, shift before my very eyes." Megan leaned forward and placed her hand over mine. "I'm sorry we jumped the gun and came in here before giving Alexei a chance to tell you himself. We weren't trying to judge you or ruin things between you and Alexei, I promise. We were just excited to meet you."

"And maybe we did want to make sure you were a nice person. We're sorry for that, too." Kerrigan smiled sheepishly.

Hannah took my other hand. "Alexei told us that you weren't like the character you played on *Love In An Instant*. And we totally believe him. We're not stupid enough to think reality TV isn't staged for dramatic effect."

I felt nauseous. "People don't shift into animals. You three are pulling my leg. I mean, you all seemed so normal and then you opened your mouths and..." But their faces told me they were dead serious and even a little regretful. "I think I'm going to throw up."

"We could prove it. We could have one of our mates shift for you and show you." Kerrigan scooted closed, not at all concerned that I might vomit on her. "I feel like your mate is the first person you should see shift, though."

I stood up, having had enough. "Don't say anything to him about you coming here."

"Not a problem." Megan groaned. "He's going to kill all three of us."

"I'm not saying I believe you, but I can't do this right now. I can't listen to this." I held up my hands when they tried to talk. "I'm sorry. Please just leave. Please."

I didn't wait to see if they'd leave. I just went to the back and hid in the employee bathroom. I bent over and braced my hands on my knees, completely thrown off by what had just happened. I'd have laughed at them and blown off what they said completely if it weren't for my prior interactions with Houdini. That was just too coincidental.

It would explain the feeling of familiarity I got when I'd looked into Alexei's eyes for the first time. What was I thinking?! There was no such thing as shapeshifters. People didn't shift into animals! There was no magic, and no fate. Just bullshit humans and their bullshit games.

Surely Alexei would have told me all this himself if it were true.

Wouldn't he? *Wait*—what if he was trying to get rid of me? Maybe this was all a ploy. He sent the three woman to Mimi's Cabana tonight to spread some weird story in the hopes that I'd drop him like a hot potato.

No, that didn't make sense either because he was the one pursuing me, not the other way around. If he wanted to get rid of me, all he had to do was say so.

For the first time in longer than I could remember, I went home early and crawled into my bed. I tried to make sense of everything as I lay there staring at the ceiling. Over and over, my mind sorted through every interaction I'd had with Alexei and with Houdini. Was it even remotely possible? A man who turns into a polar bear? I was crazy for even considering it.

When I finally did drift into a fitful sleep that night, it was only after coming to the conclusion that I would have to find out for myself. I wouldn't come right out and ask him, but there was another way. A way to test Alexei. I'd get to the bottom of what was really going on.

20

ALEXEI

I shifted into my bear in the water and hurriedly swam to Heidi that morning. I was eager to see her. I'd told her the day before that I thought we were fated to be together and I was ready to hear her thoughts about that. Maybe, if she was ready, I could explain the whole shifter thing.

She was sitting on the beach, her face blank, when I reached her. Instead of smiling and getting up to greet me with a hug the way she normally did, she just sat there. When I rubbed against her, she absently patted me on the head. She seemed a million miles away and I worried if something had happened. Maybe she'd had another nasty encounter with a diehard fan of *Love In An Instant*.

As I raged inside at the thought of someone being so rude and mean to her, she started quietly talking.

"You know what I really want, Houdini? I want a dominant man, one who tells me how it is. I've been thinking about it and as much as I like Alexei, I think he's a little too polite and respectful, you know?"

I bit back a growl. What was she talking about?

"I would be so turned on if he just pushed me around a little. If he walked up to me and said something like, 'Bitch, gimme a beer,' or grabbed me by the hair, dragged me down to my knees, and ordered me to service him. I need to be dominated—treated roughly. I don't think Alexei has that in him." She sighed. "I just feel...bored with him. We're completely mismatched."

My pride ached and my heart sank. What was my mate saying? What had changed overnight that I was suddenly boring? Had she met someone else?

She stood up and brushed the sand off her. "I'm sorry, Houdini. I wish I could hang out more this morning, but I've got to get to the boys early. Come on. I'll walk you back."

I was so thrown off that I just followed her, dumbfounded. I felt like I'd had the wind knocked out of me. She didn't even say goodbye when she knocked on the gate of that asshole Leon Zoo's place. She just turned and left.

There was something seriously wrong. She didn't seem like herself at all. Whatever was going on, I had to fix it.

I raced back to the pier, shifted and threw on my shorts before running down the beach to find her before she disappeared. I caught up to her just as she was going towards a small house right off the beach.

"Heidi!" I forced a smile and jogged up to her. "Hey. I was hoping I'd catch you again this morning."

Her expression was still flat and indifferent when she looked at me, although I thought I detected something else beneath the surface. "You caught me."

"Are you okay?"

She sighed, making it obvious that she was not okay. "Fine. Everything is fine."

I caught her hand. "Something's off. You seem different."

"I'm fine. I'm just...bored." She shrugged. "It's nothing."

Desperation can do crazy things to a man. I had no interest in pushing Heidi around or treating her "roughly", as she put it, but if that was what she wanted, hell, I'd do anything to make her happy. "If you're so bored, get on your damned knees and service me....uh...bitch."

If she'd seemed quiet, indifferent, and even bored before, she suddenly did a one eighty and her temper flared like a raging wild-fire. Her features contorted and she turned a deep shade of red before her hand shot out like a cannon and connected painfully with my face. When I jerked back, shocked, she followed me, punching me in the chest.

"Are you fucking kidding me?!"

I was so confused. "I-I'm sorry. I thought that's what you wanted! I'm sorry. Jesus, just stop punching me before you hurt yourself."

"You thought that's what I wanted? Why would you think that? Huh, Alexei? How would you know that? I didn't tell you, did I? I told a fucking polar bear!"

She was in full freak out mode, practically foaming at the mouth. When she slipped in the sand and I caught her to keep from falling, she just exploded even more. She ran down the beach still hollering.

"I've told a fucking polar bear lots of things! Lots of personal things! About how I wanted to get to know you more and then you showed up, demanding we get to know each other. I told him how hot I thought you were and how I wanted you, but I was afraid. I told him everything!"

I'd caught up to her by that point. Somehow, she'd found out I was a shifter and set me up. "Heidi..."

"Fuck you. You want to be with me, you think it's fate?" She taunted. "Bullshit. You were just feeding me what I wanted to hear. What do you really want? Just to make a complete fool of me? To fuck me and then laugh about it later? What was the point?"

I tried to grab her arms to stop her and make her listen to me, but she just smacked my hands away. "Heidi! Stop and listen to me. I'm sorry! I wasn't trying to—"

"I thought you were different. I thought you liked me." She angrily wiped away a tear. "I thought a polar bear was my friend. So, I guess this is really my fault. I was the idiot spilling my heart out to a damned bear."

"Fucking stop and listen to me. I didn't mean—"

"Go to hell." She turned and ran up the steps to her house, slamming the door so hard that the walls rattled.

I stood there, looking up at that door, feeling the pieces of my shattered heart fall to my feet. I'd fucked up. Royally.

I stayed there for a while, trying to come up with something to say, something that she'd actually want to hear, but nothing came to my mind. I'd been an idiot. I'd let her tell me everything under false pretenses. Then, I'd used that information to get closer to her.

I'd be lucky if she ever spoke to me again.

21

HEIDI

I was on day two of calling in sick to work. Hadn't showered. Hadn't brushed my teeth. Had no motivation to do either again. All my anger had faded and I was left with a terrible, depressive sadness. It just hung over my head like a cloud of doom that rained mopiness on me. I wanted anger back, because at least with anger came motivation. Motivation to lash out at Alexei, or spend time visualizing kicking him in the balls, but still. With sadness, I just wanted to lay on my bed and stare at the ceiling. Or worse, cry.

Alexei was exactly why I'd stayed away from men since moving to Sunkissed Key. The whole situation was. Dreaming of something I couldn't have sucked. I hadn't felt so lonely before Alexei. I hadn't stayed in bed all day long and cried over the realization that no one was ever going to touch me again. Alexei. Alexei was never going to touch me again.

It was awful how I still wanted him. The anger had faded but thoughts of him were still driving me crazy. I didn't understand how he'd managed to get past all my defenses so thoroughly, but he had.

He was well and truly under my skin.

I missed Houdini... who was really Alexei. The whole concept was still insane to me. Alexei turned into a bear and...what? Sat and listened to women talk so he could find out their inner thoughts, and then use them to lure the women into bed? No, that made no sense. Alexei didn't need any tricks to get a woman into bed. He probably got propositioned daily. Well, whatever his reason for doing it, I did miss stroking his fur while I chatted away. I missed curling up against him and watching the ocean roll in over the sand and then back out.

I wasn't stupid. I knew I sounded like an idiot, crying over a lost friendship with a bear. Was I so lonely and pitiful that I thought a bear was my friend? The answer was sad.

I hadn't even begun to process what it meant that he could shift from man to bear. I just wasn't there.

I was still feeling hurt over the betrayal.

Had Alexei been laughing the entire time he'd been using what I told him to lure me in? Had I been such an easy target? I felt like I was going to be shamed and ridiculed all over again, even more. I'd dragged him into the back of the bar and had an orgasm against an old rickety desk. People were going to know I'd done that. They were going to feel like they were right in their judgements of me.

I was really working myself into a big crying spell when someone knocked on my front door. I cringed.

I knew it wasn't Maria. She'd asked her mother to step in and look after the kids for a couple days after I'd given her a brief rundown of why I'd gone into hiding. She knew better than to come over until I asked her to. Maria was the only person who ever stopped over, so... was it Alexei? I wasn't ready to face him. Especially not all smelly and gross and in the same clothes I'd worn for the past two days. I didn't want him to know how he'd affected me.

"It's us! Megan, Hannah, and Kerrigan. The relationship-ruiners."

I fell back into bed, planning on ignoring them. They'd go away eventually.

"We aren't leaving, Heidi. You're stuck with us on your porch until you let us in."

I groaned. "Go away!"

"No, ma'am." Evidently, Megan was their stubborn ringleader. "We'll camp out here if we have to."

The only reason I got up was so I could throw something at her. I scrunched my face into my best scowl and jerked open the door. "Go away. I don't want to see you. Any of you."

Megan shrugged and pushed her way past me. "Well, I suppose you'll have to get over it. We're not going anywhere."

Kerrigan moved past me next. "I like your house. It's cute."

When Hannah just stood there, a stupid smile on her face, I stepped aside. "Well. You might as well join your pals."

She patted my arm as she moved past. "I'm sorry we're barging in like this. We have to, though. We messed up and we owe it to you and Alexei to stage an intervention."

"Don't say his name."

Megan turned away from a picture of me with the boys and faced me. "Alexei, Alexei, Alexei. You'd best get used to it because you're going to be hearing a lot of his name today and for the rest of your life. We have a lot to explain. Where should we set up? And would you like to shower first?"

I gave her an incredulous look.

She laughed. "Okay, no shower."

Hannah groaned. "I'm so sorry. We're all so sorry. Megan doesn't mean to be so rude, but we've been watching Alexei mope around like his world came to an end. He's so sad and it's all our fault."

"Oh, your fault, huh? Were you the ones who told him to convince me that he was a polar bear escaped from the local animal sanctuary? You told him to sit and listen to me pour my heart out about this really hot guy I met? You told him to use the information to get me to agree to go out with him?"

Kerrigan whistled. "No one ever claimed he was the sharpest tool in the shed."

"He *is* the sweetest, though. He's not a bad guy, Heidi. He's just... clueless. He should've known better, yes. He should've done some things differently. He didn't, though. And it doesn't change that he's your mate and that the two of you are fated to be together." Megan put her hands on her hips. "Now, how about that shower?"

I scowled. "Rude, much?"

She shook her head. "You'll forgive us later."

"Doubt it."

"I'm really going to enjoy being friends with you when all of this is over. I'm always saying how these two are just too nice."

"You really just bullied your way into my house and are insulting me. Nice."

She just grinned. "You're going to enjoy us being friends, too. I mean, after you forgive me for all of this."

22

ALEXEI

I'd never felt worse in my life. I missed Heidi more than I thought possible. My chest ached. I was usually the most laid back of the team. Things didn't often ruffle my feathers, but this —my bear was slowly losing his shit and so was I. My world was falling apart. I'd even gotten my nose broken on the job by a nutcase rabbit shifter with a few too many beers in him who didn't want to be calmed. I didn't even know rabbit shifters existed. He'd gotten the drop on me and it would have been more than a little embarrassing except I didn't care about anything but my mate.

I'd gone to the beach every morning waiting for Heidi, but she never showed. She was making it more than clear that she didn't want anything to do with me. I got it. I'd pulled some stupid shit.

I should've come clean sooner, before she found out herself. I shouldn't have used what she told me to try to win her over. I shouldn't have let her spill her private info without letting her know it was me she was spilling it to not some dumb animal. Although right now, I supposed that description could accurately be applied to me—dumb animal.

I'd been pissed at Megan, Kerrigan, and Hannah at first for flapping their gums and assuming Heidi knew everything. They'd just dropped the whole thing on her like a bomb. They had to have freaked her out beyond belief. It wasn't really their fault, though. Not really. I'd been the idiot.

"How's the nose?"

I looked up at Serge and shrugged. "Fine. Healed already."

He chose the chair opposite me in the office, and sank into it with a grunt. "You okay?"

Frowning, I looked away. "Not really."

"She'll come around. It's just the way it works."

I wasn't so sure. I'd tricked her. I'd taken away the chance for her to want to tell me, the man, everything. "Sure."

"Hannah and the other two went over there yesterday." He grunted again. "Figured they'd try to repair what they'd broken."

I sat up straighter. "What happened?"

"They all argued a lot, apparently. Your mate isn't very trusting, it seems." He laughed. "Hannah said she's stubborn and is the perfect mate for you because you need someone strong enough to deal with your shit."

The ache in my chest grew stronger. "She has plenty of reason to not trust people."

"So, I hear."

I stood up and went to the window. There were people walking past on the street, but no one that I wanted to see. "Did they say how it all ended?"

"I got the impression that they weren't done talking to her."

"I should've been the one telling her everything."

"Well, it's too late for that now. So, you can either feel shitty about yourself, or you can go and fix it."

Frowning at him, I held my hands up in the air. "How? How do I fix it?"

"Not by sitting here and feeling sorry for yourself."

"I don't feel sorry for myself. I feel sorry for what I did to her. There's a difference." I shoved my hands in my hair and tugged. "I fucking miss her. It feels like part of me is dying."

Serge walked over to me and put his hand on my shoulder. "Make it right. You can do it. We've all been where you are, wondering how the fuck we're going to get our mates back. With Hannah, I thought I was going to fucking choke on the pain."

"I don't know what to do. I lost her trust. She fucking hates me, man. No big gesture is going to fix that."

He squeezed my shoulder and then let go. "Don't try for big gesture then. You're smart. You'll figure it out. She's your mate. You're literally made for her. Stop bellyaching in here and go get your mate back. You're on leave until you do. I need you on the team, but last night was bad. You could've been hurt. You could've gotten the team hurt."

I growled. "Serge, I have to work. I can't just...do nothing."

"Don't do nothing then, asshole. Go get your mate."

I watched him leave and sank back into my chair. I didn't know what to do. I didn't know how to make it right after breaking her trust. I couldn't think through the haze of pain.

Sitting there for the rest of the day, I was finally so stiff from not moving that I forced myself to get up and go out. I walked down the beach, no real aim in mind. At least, that's what I thought until I saw that I was outside of Heidi's house.

I had no plan. I needed to think of something before I tried to talk to her, but still, I walked up to her door and knocked. She didn't answer and I couldn't smell her sweet scent close by. I sank onto the top step and deflated. I felt like I was barely holding on. I needed her.

"Alexei?"

I looked up and saw Megan coming towards me. I couldn't pretend like I wasn't broken to save face, so I just shrugged and stared out at the ocean view that Heidi had. It was beautiful, but I couldn't truly appreciate it.

"Oh, Alexei." Megan sat next to me and sighed. "I'm so sorry that we did this."

"Not your fault."

"Some of it's our fault." She nudged me with her elbow. "She's going to come around."

I wasn't so sure.

"Just talk to her. Come clean about everything and put yourself out there. Show her your vulnerable side." She stood up. "She's stubborn, but she'll hear you eventually."

I just nodded and kept my eyes trained on the ocean.

"Ugh. You bears are all the same. You think you're so strong, but you're just lost little cubs without your mate." She patted me on the head. "Get your mate, little cub, before you melt away in a puddle of sadness."

"Too late."

She just laughed. "If you don't make some sort of effort soon, she's going to think you don't care."

I finally looked at her. "I care more than I care about anything else in the world."

"Well, act like it. This feeling sorry for yourself isn't solving anything."

I grunted. "You and Serge are pains."

"Yeah, well. So are you."

23

HEIDI

I didn't want to be at work, but I could only shirk my responsibilities for so long. My tips were going to be pitiful tonight since the only expression I could manage was a frown, but it wasn't fair to Mimi and Sarah to have to cover my shift for yet another might.

My mind was elsewhere and I kept screwing up drinks. I couldn't help it. All the things the trio of women had told me were running through my head on a continual loop. The women turned out to not be so bad. They were rather nice, really. But, the info they gave me...wow!

Polar bears and shifters of every kind existed. Men who shifted into animals, did whatever they wanted to do as animals, and then shifted back to men. It was mind blowing. And all true. I'd watched Megan's mate shift. They hadn't wanted to show me, but I insisted. If they expected me to believe something so off the wall, I needed to see it with my own eyes.

Not that I didn't halfway believe it already. That stupid test I'd put Alexei through had proven that he knew exactly what I told Houdini. I mean, what I'd told Alexei. As Houdini. Since they were one in the same.

I dropped a glass of ice and swore. It was going to be a long night. I would get over it and move on at some point. No matter what the women said. They seemed to be convinced that nothing would get better for me until I talked to Alexei. I wasn't ready for that, though. I still felt like such a fool. I'd opened myself—raw and exposed—never knowing I was spilling my innermost feelings to a man I'd just met and hardly knew. I mean, how the hell could I possible have known?

"You okay?" Sarah leaned over the bar, her worry evident. "You look like you're a million miles away."

I swept the broken glass and melting ice into the dustpan and tossed the whole mess into the trash. "I'm okay. Everything's okay."

"Mimi and I can do without you, if you need to go home. You look like you're barely holding it together." She ducked under the bar and came up to me. "It's obvious you're going through something, Heidi. Go home if you need to. You work hard for this place and no one is going to be mad if you need a little more personal time for whatever you're going through."

I blinked back tears and swallowed down the lump in my throat. "I actually do need a minute to myself."

She sighed and straightened my hair. "Okay, just...take a break. I don't know what's going on with you, but you look like seconds from an all-out sob fest."

She had no clue how right she was. As though I hadn't indulged in enough sob fests already.

I took a five-minute break in the back and when I came out, I was a little more together and could at least pretend on the outside like I wasn't such a wreck inside. Things were going better until I dropped another glass. This time, it shattered into the ice. Swearing, I braced myself on the bar and took a deep breath.

"Heidi?"

I glanced up at Sarah and shook my head. "I have to change this ice out."

I'd just gotten started pouring pitchers of warm water over the ice when a couple of guys settled themselves at the bar in front of me. I glanced up and tossed them an absent smile before going back to my chore of melting the ice.

"Ahem. Are you going to take our order?"

I strained to keep my faux smile in place. "Yes. It'll be just a minute. I'm in the middle of something. Sorry about this."

I went back to cleaning out the ice, making sure everything melted, drained and was cleaned, ensuring no glass shards were inadvertently sent out in someone's drink. I was just about finished when I realized the men were snickering.

My back instantly stiffened. I'd had snickers like that directed at me plenty of times over the years. They were never good. I looked up to find them recording me while I was bent over, working. Scowling, I turned to face them. "What the fuck is wrong with you?"

"Whoa, sweetheart. We were just enjoying the view. It's not a big deal." The guy with the phone put it down and rolled his eyes. "It's not like you're not used to it."

I had a job to keep, a level of professionalism I needed to uphold. That night, though, I couldn't calm down. I was pissed, all the anger and sadness I'd been feeling finally had a solid outlet.

"Keep your eyes and your camera to yourself or I'll break them both, you skinny little shit." I glared at both of them. "You can leave now. I'm not serving either of you."

Phone boy scowled back at me. "You don't have to be a bitch. Jesus."

"And you don't have to act like a creep."

"Fuck you." He looked down at me like I was something gross he'd stepped in. "It's not like either of us really wanted to look at a piece of trash like you. Everyone knows you've been around the block so many times that you'll spread your legs for any Tom or Harry... oops, I mean Dick!" His buddy laughed like that was actually funny.

"Get out." My hand reacted before my mind did, but I wasn't sorry that I threw a pitcher of warm water at him.

He was drenched, water pooling in his lap until he jumped up and tried to shake it off. His face was beet red and his expression said he wanted to strangle me. "You bitch!"

Sarah came rushing over, her eyes wide. "You okay, Heidi?"

"Is *she* okay? That bitch just poured water on me. I want to talk to your manager!"

"Call her a bitch one more time and you'll be scraping your jaw off the floor."

The deep timbre of Alexei's voice startled me, but it was nothing compared to how I felt when I looked at him and saw the dark expression on his face as he stared down the two men. His hair was disheveled, he was unshaven, and there were dark circles under his eyes. He looked rough. I got a sick satisfaction out of realizing that he'd been as miserable as I'd been.

"Fuck off, asshole. This doesn't involve you."

"That's where you're wrong. She's mine and you're a dead man if you keep talking to her like that."

Sarah held up her hands and moved between the two men. "Okay, that's enough. No one's fighting in here."

"So, your sorry ass got stuck with her? How does it feel to know your woman has been passed around like a bad cold?"

Alexei growled low in his throat. "Excuse me."

I watched with widening eyes as he picked Sarah up and placed her back on her feet behind him as though he were relocating a figurine. She gasped at what she saw behind her, but before Alexei could turn back around, the asshole with the cell phone swung his fist out and hit Alexei in the side of the head.

He really shouldn't have done that.

24

HEIDI

Alexei picked up the offending asshole like he weighed nothing and easily tossed him overhead towards the exit. The guy hit the door sideways, and tumbled onto the floor. "I'm letting you go. Make the right choice."

Asshole's friend swallowed so loudly that I heard it from where I was standing. "I don't want any trouble."

"Take your friend and get the fuck out, then."

Cell phone guy who was climbing to his feet wasn't nearly as smart as his buddy, though. "Fuck you and your ho bitch, man." This scene was going to get even bigger, apparently, because he then focused his gaze on me. "Everyone in here knows who you are! Everyone saw you on national television, fucking every guy with a pulse."

The bar had gone quiet, except for the music which was oddly loud without the buzz of conversation. It was painfully obvious that everyone was listening to what was going on and all eyes were on us.

I wanted to sink behind the bar and never come out again. Not only did I want to, I actually did it. I couldn't face everyone. It was one thing when I had to deal with people one on one, or two on one. A whole bar full of people was too much. I slid down behind the bar, my back to the bucket of ice that I'd been cleaning out, and wrapped my arms around my legs. It wasn't my proudest moment, but I needed to get away.

"What kind of moron are you?" Alexei's voice was raised, his anger palpable. "That shit isn't real. It was all staged—completely fake. Everyone on the show followed a script. She was cast as the villain and did her job the way she was supposed to. But, even if it wasn't all phony, that gives you no right to treat her like an object. Your vile behavior shows *your* character not hers."

Sarah's voice rose, too. "Yeah, you're the only trash here. You and anyone else who would harass someone based on what you saw on TV show almost a decade ago."

"She's a better person than you could ever hope to be. She's kind, smart, and caring. You'd be lucky to kiss her feet." Alexei growled. "Which isn't going to happen. She's mine. Even if I'll never deserve her either."

Mimi's voice rose from the back. "Okay, boys, this has gone on long enough. If you have an issue with one of my bartenders because you think you have the upper hand on some gossip about them, stay the hell away. Take your money somewhere else. Like back to the hole you crawled out of." I really loved my boss, Mimi.

"Yeah!" Sarah cheered along.

I heard Alexei's low, strong voice next. "I suggest you leave now of your own volition. If not, I will make you leave—now. One of those options ends with you in traction, eating your meals through a straw for the next six months. Your choice."

I listened with strained ears, but I couldn't hear anything. I couldn't figure out what was happening until the door slammed and people cheered. Then Sarah's head appeared over the top of the bar and her grin stretched as wide as her face.

"They're gone." She reached over and stroked my hair.

Mimi rounded the bar and stood in front of me. "You okay, honey?"

I shook my head and then nodded. "Yeah. No. I don't know."

"I think the hottie has a real thing for you! Did you hear him?" Sarah sighed, still hanging over the bar. "He said you're *his*."

Mimi's hand flew to her chest. "He's not the type a girl should let slip through her fingers. Trust me on that. I know. I've been married five times."

I forced a smile and pulled myself up. She was right. No more hiding. I had to talk to Alexei and at least thank him for standing up for me. When I turned, though, he was gone.

Sarah sighed. "Where'd he go?"

I looked around the bar. People were staring at me, but the looks were curious rather than cruel. The vibe in Mimi's Cabana quickly returned to normal, the drama forgotten, but Alexei was nowhere to be seen.

"I should thank him."

Mimi snorted. "You should marry him."

I groaned. "Things are more complicated than that."

"Oh, really? A man that beautiful wants you and is willing to fight for you and it's complicated? Okay. Complicated. Sure."

I stood up taller and scanned the place once more hoping to find him. "It's more than just that. He...he did some stuff."

Sarah's eyes widened. "He cheated?"

"No."

Mimi crossed her arms over her large chest and coconut bra. "He's abusive?"

"No."

Mimi nodded knowingly. "He's only into anal."

I jerked around to face her. "No! What's wrong with you?"

She laughed. "Then, it sounds like whatever he did is forgivable. Go, get him."

"I..." I blew out a shaky breath and looked for him again. "It's—"

"Take a chance," Sarah said. "You've lived like a nun the entire time you've been here. It's time for you go a little wild."

I looked at the door and wondered where he'd gone. "I don't like the consequences of living wildly."

"Maybe the outcome will be in your favor this time. How will you know if you don't take that chance? Now, go. I can't stand here and convince you to do what's best for you all night long. I've got tables to wait."

As I stood there after Sarah went back to work and tried to think through what I was going to do, Mimi took over pouring drinks. I could stay and let him get on with his life. We could both go back to the way things were. I'd forget him eventually, no matter what Megan and the other women said, and live the rest of my life the way I had been.

So, things weren't exciting? So, I was lonely? At least I was safe.

Or I could step out of my comfort zone and go after him—let him explain. We might even be able to work things out. Maybe the women were right and he was my mate and things would never be fine again because they'd be amazing.

"Two beers, please!"

I climbed over the bar, and ran out the door amidst cheers of the patrons who had been side eying me, second guessing what I was gonna do. Well, what I was gonna do was hear Alexei out. But, that was all. I deserved an explanation. Yeah, that was the only reason I was chasing him down.

25

ALEXEI

I crossed Main Street and walked to the beach. I was barely holding myself together, anger getting the best of me. I wanted to lash out and rip someone's head off. I wanted to hurt everyone who'd ever hurt Heidi, including myself.

The image of her crouching behind the bar, hiding, was scorched into my brain. I couldn't unsee it. She was hurt. She deserved better. I wanted to be the one who made it all better, yet I'd only made it worse for her.

I shifted, not concerned about my shredded clothing, and padded into the water. My bear was mourning the loss of his mate, his sorrow audible as he cried. We were both mourning. It was my fault. I hadn't taken things seriously enough and I'd ruined everything.

"Alexei!"

I turned towards the sound of my name being called and froze. Running toward the water was Heidi. She stopped at the water's edge and stepped out of her shoes before wading into the water.

"We have to talk. Right now." Out of breath, she was waist deep in the water, the bottom of her dress floating up around her hips.

I swam closer, still keeping my distance, and just waited. Had she really chased after me?

"I want to hear what you have to say. I need to hear it. Can you shift back?"

My bear retreated, leaving me there to face what I'd done. I swam closer to our mate and felt my stomach twist painfully. "I'm sorry."

Her eyes were wide and she blinked a few times. "Wow."

"I know. That doesn't really cut it, does it? I am, though. I'm sorry I wasn't honest with you. I should've told you right away. I should've shown you and let you decide what you wanted to tell me. It was yours to decide and I took that away from you. I know how wrong I was."

"You make it look so easy."

"What?"

She stepped closer. "Shifting. I saw Roman do it, but it's not the same. It's amazing. You're a bear one second and then you're...you. Wow...it's so...beautiful."

I stilled. "You think it's beautiful?"

She nodded. "Can you do it again? Right now?"

I wasn't going to tell her no. I shifted into my bear and chuffed at her. I was amazed when she smiled and held her hand out for me to come closer. I eased closer, but I let her decide if she wanted to touch me. I was done presuming things.

She scratched behind my ears the way I liked. "Again, please."

I shifted back and stared down at her. Her hand cupped the side of my face and I pressed my cheek into her palm greedily. "I'm sorry, Heidi."

"Did you mean to trick me? Was it supposed to be a joke?"

I shook my head. "I never meant to trick you in a bad way. At first, before I realized you were my mate, I thought it would be funny for a polar bear to be on a beach in Florida. But after that, it was just... me...hanging out with you any way I could. It was wrong of me, though, not to provide you with full disclosure."

"You think I'm your mate?"

I held her gaze. "I know you are. Everything about you calls to me. I meant what I said about fate. I understand you being angry. I knew I wasn't making the best choices, but I was so desperate to be with you that I didn't care. I should've thought things through."

"Megan told me that shifters need their mates. She said that you would be in physical pain without me."

I just nodded.

"And you were just going to leave and let me shut you out?"

I nodded again. "I'm not going to force you to be with me. I've done enough."

"So, what? You just suffer?"

"It's fine, Heidi. You don't owe me anything. Don't worry about me, okay?"

She stepped closer, the water up to her chest then. "You said you're sorry."

"I am. Very much."

"I forgive you." She came even closer. "I think..."

"What? What do you think?"

She let out a shaky laugh. "I'm terrified. I'm terrified that you might hurt me again. I want to believe all of the mate stuff, but it's not easy. It's been a long time since I've been able to believe the best of something."

Too eagerly, I moved closer to her. "I can show you. I can show you that you're bound to me and that we're meant to be together."

"How?"

I trailed my finger down her neck. "The mark. You'll feel what I feel. You'll know that this is real. It's serious, though. It's forever after that. There's no going back."

"You want to mark me?"

"So badly that my bones ache from it. If you're not ready, though, it's okay. We can go slowly. We can—"

"Alexei?"

"Yeah?"

"Stop talking and do it." She closed the gap between us and put her finger to my lips. "But then we both let it go. I forgive you. You have to forgive yourself, too. I'm not fragile. I don't need you apologizing and treating me like I'm going to break. I want you the way you are."

My hands went to her waist and I sucked in a sharp breath. "Can I talk?"

"I guess."

"I want to mark you as mine. I want to claim you so there's never a doubt that you belong to me and that I belong to you. No games, no jokes, just you and me, together."

She sighed and swayed into me. "Forever?"

"If there's anything longer than forever, then that."

"You won't change your mind?"

"Heidi?"

"Yeah?"

"Stop talking and let me do it."

26

HEIDI

I gasped as Alexei pulled me into his body and kissed me. God, the man could kiss. He made love to my mouth in a way that I'd never experienced. His lips moved over mine slowly and deliberately, tasting and teasing. He moved from my bottom lip to my top lip before running his tongue over them, seeking entrance.

I was a puddle as he stroked my lips and then my tongue. Short and teasing strokes built up to strong, deep strokes that drove me crazy. I couldn't get enough of his kisses.

I wrapped myself around him, longing for more. Locking my arms around his neck and my legs around his waist, I felt the thick ridge of his erection press against my core.

Alexei growled against my mouth and pulled back to look at me. "Fuck, you're beautiful like this, with lips red and swollen from my kisses and your pulse beating like crazy at the base of your throat."

I kissed his neck and ran my tongue over his skin, tasting him. "When are you going to mark me?"

He groaned and I felt his erection pulse against me. "Are you sure, mate?"

I liked hearing him call me that. I liked it a lot. "Yes. I want you to mark me. Will you be able to see it? When you look at me, will you see that I'm yours?"

Another pulse. "You're killing me. It'll be visible. All shifters will know. I'll feel you, too. We'll feel each other—through the bond."

"Do you know what you'd feel right now? If you could feel me?" I ran my fingers through his hair and peppered kisses on his lips. "You'd feel that I don't want to wait anymore. I want you—now."

He swore and his mouth descended over mine again as he pivoted us. The pier where we'd first met was behind him, and he pressed my back against it. We weren't immersed so deeply that the water covered us completely, but we were far enough out that were cloaked by darkness.

Alexei pinned me to the thick wooden pillar with his lower body and slid the top of my dress down over my shoulders and even farther, taking my strapless bra with it. As the waves rolled in, the cool water kissed my bared breasts seconds before his mouth did.

With lingering strokes of his tongue and deep, hungry, open mouthed kisses to them, he only stopped when I pulled his head up and silently begged him for more. The blue of his eyes were glowing a bright sliver in the moonlight. "What's the magic word?"

I dropped my head back as his hand trailed down my side and worked its way between us. When my panties were shoved aside and his thick finger was easing into me, we both moaned.

I reached up and behind me to grab the pier, trying desperately to brace myself against something firm and solid. I was light-headed and had the feeling that I was floating away. "Alexei, more."

He slid another finger into me and ran his tongue over my breasts again, sucking and nibbling. He was purposefully driving me crazy. "Say the magic word and I'll take you right now. I'll make you scream my name and mark you as mine. All you have to do is say it."

"Please!"

He grinned, resting his forehead against mine as he pumped his fingers back and forth and his thumb swiped over my clit sending shivers of pleasure through my body. "That's a good one and we may use it later, but it's not the magic word I want to hear from you."

And suddenly, I knew exactly the word he was waiting for. He was waiting for a concrete confirmation. "Mate...you're my mate. You're mine, Alexei, and I want you in me."

He groaned and then his fingers were gone and in their place a crushing emptiness. But, before I could voice a protest, his cock was there instead, slowly filling me until I thought I couldn't handle another inch.

He gripped the pier, his hand partly over mine, and his other hand cupped my ass. His forehead pressed to mine, eyes focused on me, as he slowly moved. His hips gyrated with the gentle rocking of the waves, pumping in and out of me in a rhythm that sent me reeling.

I watched the strain on his handsome face, the way he held back, and wanted desperately to see him let go and lose control. I arched my back and met his thrusts harder. I used my hands, locked around the pier, to give me leverage to increase the friction between our bodies.

My move seemed to have its intended effect. He swore and thrust into me harder and faster, matching my pace. His grip on my ass was bruising. "I'm not going to last long like this, Heidi."

"Good. I want you to come with me." I shuddered, my body close to coming apart for him. "Mark me. Mark me, mate."

That was all that he needed. He used his chin to nudge my head to the side and then his tongue stroked over my exposed neck. I held my breath, but he just licked me again.

"*Mate.*" I moaned. "Please!"

He let out a wild snarl and then sank his teeth into my neck. It hurt for only a split second before the pleasure hit full force. It seemed to come from all directions and all at once. My body tightened... and then snapped with an orgasm unlike any I'd ever felt flowing over me, I trembled like an earthquake, the contractions rocking me to the core. The pleasure radiated, going out, coming back in, rolling through me. Everywhere.

And I screamed, lost somewhere in a blissful euphoria, not caring who heard, I screamed Alexei's name.

Alexei thrust a few more strokes and then went still, buried in me to the hilt. I felt his seed filling me, as another orgasm started up for me, even stronger, as though his climax had triggered mine. The sounds I made were helpless cries of surrender to a passion more powerful than I thought possible.

I wasn't sure how long we hung onto the pier like that, but the moon was higher in the sky when I was able to think clearly again. I opened my eyes to find Alexei watching me, a crooked grin on his face. "What?"

He bit his lip and that smile grew wider. "You're mine."

I couldn't help but smile back. I felt...him, his emotions toward me. An overwhelming sense of pride and warmth and joy...and love. I could feel through our bond the depth of his feelings for me. I held his face in my hands and tasted his lips, hoping he also knew through the bond what I thought of him.

Fate had given me a gift, for whatever reason, and I wasn't one to be ungrateful.

"Alexei, let's go back to my house. I want to hear *you* say please. Magic words work both ways, you know?"

He laughed and pulled me away from the pier. He insisted on carrying me up the beach and then up the stairs to my house. Anyone looking out their window would've gotten quite the view.

"You're not into just anal, right?"

He stumbled. "What?"

"Sorry, sorry. It was something that Mimi said." I hesitated. "I'm willing to experiment, just as long as it's not all anal, all the time."

"Stop saying anal."

"I'm just checking."

"Okay, well, no, I'm not into all anal, all the time."

I laughed as he tried to carry me into the bathroom while looking for the bedroom. "Next room on the right."

He found it and dropped me on the bed.

I pulled him down on top of me and kissed him. "Wait."

He stiffened. "What?"

"Why was Mr. Zoo just accepting a random polar bear into his animal sanctuary?"

"It's a long story."

"No wonder he was so rude to me." I laughed. "I kept bringing him an animal that he didn't want."

Alexei buried his face in my shoulder and growled. "Enough talking about another man. In fact, let's stop talking altogether."

I tangled my hands in his hair and shifted my hips so he brushed against my entrance. "I could talk about anal some more."

He laughed and sank into me in one deep thrust. "Heidi?"

"Yeah?"

"Please."

NEXT BOOK: **Tactical Bear**

For more books, please visit:

https://books2read.com/candaceayers

https://lovestruckromance.com

Candace Ayers ♡

Made in the USA
Coppell, TX
08 July 2023

18877530R00073